Chapter One

One of her first feelings about him, a full hour before she had fallen in love with Charles Masters, or even met him, was how enormously more grown-up he must be than she was. Not merely older; she took that as read. Indeed, when they actually met, his youthfulness was a surprise. Not merely older, but so much further on.

What disconcerted her, as she made her way to the interview and crossed London eastwards, was the thought that, in terms of achievement, of actually doing something with life, she had hardly advanced at all. She was twenty-seven and this was the first paid employment, apart from casual vacation jobs, for which she had ever applied.

She was leaving her university world, her library world, for a place where real decisions were made, real money earned, a place of offices, or diary appointments and secretaries. Mr Masters could see her at ten, she had been told at first. Then, no. It would be better to make it ten fifteen; but could she come a little early, in case he was available? He had to conduct an important interview with counsel at eleven.

Counsel – or the council? Both would have been very

much the same to her; that is, in common with so much in this city and this country, a mystery. She was to make her way to Bishopsgate. A book of maps called *A to Z*, pronounced zed, saw to that; but then, having collected a pass from a janitor, she was to proceed to the eighth floor.

This was what a grown-up life so often was. It was all so much what a dad would do when, briefcase in hand, he kissed his wife and children and left the house. Hence her interview, since a dad was what he was, though evidently a dad too busy to have much to do with the children. He clearly needed her, or someone like her, to help him out of a difficulty. Even so, he could not easily fit her into the busy schedule.

If anyone had wanted to see her, Sallie Declan, no such hoo-ha would have been necessary. All she would have had to do, if someone required her attention, was to switch off the laptop. No appointments needed to be made. No secretaries, no janitors, no passes, no elevators were required to find your way to the slightly appalling bedsit in Hackney she rented from the friend of a friend.

Even the word 'friend', since she came to London would have to be put in inverted commas if you were speaking the truth. There were fellow grads in the overpriced Hall of Residence where she had stayed for her first few months. There were a few with whom she occasionally met for coffee and discussed their eternal theme: how the thesis was doing. But she painfully missed the Group, whom she had left behind at Carver, Ohio. She missed the jokes. She missed the sense of belonging not merely to a set, but to the clever set. The Group, self-consciously so called, had no obvious Mary McCarthy, but they were the ones at Carver who would know who Mary McCarthy was. What an avalanche of jokes, what a host of little ironies, had pursued her when she had first mooted the idea of putting in for this scholarship and coming to England!

Inevitably, given her thesis subject, the jokes had mostly revolved around herself as a Jamesian heroine, an 'innocent' American, let loose among the social complexities and moral duplicities of old Europe.

In fact, she had only been to one English home in the seven or eight months she had been here. It had been kindly meant, on Professor Helstone's part, to invite her to his modest establishment in Wimbledon, shared with a wife and two grown-up daughters. Sunday lunches there had provided their glacial equivalent of home life, but they had hardly qualified as Isabel Archer falling into the wily clutches of Madame Merle. Conversation had been a little stilted, with the professor chatting amiably but boringly about faculty business and Mrs Helstone being a bit embarrassing. Sallie had disliked the way the professor's wife had adopted such an apologetic tone when discussing the latest developments in international affairs. 'I'm afraid we did not really approve . . . I hope you won't take this the wrong way, but we thought your president should never . . .'

As if Sallie, or any of the Group, could stand the president! His policies were an anathema. Surely the professor's wife could see that no *intelligent* Americans, no persons like Sallie herself, adopted the hawkish views that were being, so tentatively, criticised?

It would have been difficult to know how the great American novelist would have conveyed the Helstones' ménage or their table, the slightly indigestible pulses, wild rice and rubbery breads offered with such limited friendliness. Mrs Headway could hardly have embarked upon her 'Siege of London' from such a vantage point as the Helstones' kitchen-diner. No invitations to stay at grand house parties and no dinner parties at which one might meet an Italian prince had come Sallie's way. While she was still living in the dormitory block in Bloomsbury, there had been, on the boy's part, an attempt at a love affair. He was a New Zealander, working on an aspect of metallurgy upon which Sallie found it hard, when he spoke of it, to concentrate. After the Christmas, for which she had gone home, there had been no resumption of that relationship, or non-relationship.

Home was a suburb of Muncie, Indiana, or that was where her mom had fetched up. Sallie was an only child. She had been born, a fact which sparkled when revealed in the right company, in Defiance. Her dad, who worked as a manager in an electrical firm, moved them all to Chicago when he got his big break. That was when she was about five. She had started her nursery school in a suburb of Chicago, while her dad's job, now so important that it involved travelling, was still able to pay for a double garage, a big garden, even dreams of a swimming pool. She was eight when her mom, tearfully and hurriedly, took her back to Defiance. Sometimes, when Mom herself was trying to establish a new relationship, Sallie had been sent like a parcel back to Chicago to stay with her dad. Dad's new girlfriend had children with whom Sallie had never gotten on. Dad veered between guilt-ridden over-attention to Sallie, hugging and even crying over her, and the desire to appease his new wife by strictness and coldness towards the little girl. Eventually, things got so bad between her parents – and the fights about arrangements, holidays, who had the kid which weekend got so bad – that she just hung around with Mom. Visits to Dad got rarer. It was actually some years since she had even seen the man. Her career since high school – her BA at the decent, Midwestern college of Shaker Oakes, the MA at Carver, Ohio, and the scholarship to do a doctorate in England – was a story she had not bothered to tell, nor he to read or hear.

For much of childhood, then, solitude had been natural to her. Solitude at home, with her own small back bedroom with its stuffed animals and childhood books and miniature television, or even her solitude at Shaker Oakes and before friendships had been formed, had not prepared her for the crushing loneliness of London.

The graduate dorm in Bloomsbury did nothing to dispel the loneliness, with its smell of trainers and disinfectant, its scruffy common room, its population of African, Australian, Canadian and American seekers after abstruse knowledge and doctoral reward. She found the company was not to her taste and, despite the apparent generosity of the scholarship, she found life in London cripplingly expensive. It was also very frightening. The area just north of her hostel, around King's Cross station, was haunted by hookers and junkies, and she scarcely liked to go there to catch the Tube even in daylight hours. A Tube ride, in suffocating crowds and filthy trains, cost three dollars for quite short journeys. The initial impulses of her late-September arrival – the thought that she would get to know the great capital, visit its museums and galleries, attend concerts, make interesting friendships with amusing English people – had faded by Christmas time.

Nevertheless, it had been a great mistake, leaving the graduate hostel. Somehow, she had thought that Hackney, her present address, sounded more homey than Bloomsbury. And it was the chance, offered by a postcard pinned to the noticeboard in her Hall of Residence, of belonging to a 'friendly non-smoking household' that made her go for it. She'd hoped 'friendly' meant eating together, or at least, sometimes, talking. The household did not, as she had supposed, have communal mealtimes. Three or four others, similarly situated, inhabited bedsits in the chilly little property and no one seemed to have worked out a sched for whose turn it was to clean the kitchen or throw away the sour milk in the fridge.

In the course of January she had sunk from mild gloom into actual depression. Why had she ever supposed that writing a Ph.D. thesis was a good way of spending her twenties? This was surely meant to be the liveliest, free-est decade of a woman's existence? The responsibilities of adulthood, marriage, children lay in the future. The constraints of childhood lay behind her. Sometimes she looked despondently around the reading room of the British Library and asked inwardly – what are we all doing here when we could be living? It was a very Jamesian question, of course. Strether, in *The Ambassadors*, urges Little Bilham to 'Live all you can, it's a mistake not to'. It was a mistake he'd made himself, not living. Maybe living was just too dangerous, too frightening? Her parents had certainly not made a very good stab at it. The jobs by which grown-ups became enslaved were for the most part boring or immoral. Postpone, postpone. That was why she, and so many others, were doing first a Masters, then a doctorate. It was a useful way of postponing the knowledge that life was not going to bring many rewards, or laughs.

She saw them, her kind, as the twenty-first-century equivalent of the medieval wandering scholars who traipsed from university to university or monastery to monastery, clutching their twenty *bokes* of Aristotle, like Chaucer's Clerk. The pilgrimages were notionally quests for know-ledge, but for the most part they were flights from boring jobs and families.

During this low, and very depressed, phase she returned to the graduate common room, just in the hope of making friends. She started attending lectures and in this way she picked up a handful of acquaintances, most of them fellow Americans. These, if glimpsed in the library, could at least relieve her loneliness by giving her a smile and a wave; with one of them, a girl called Kate from Connecticut, she even had the occasional cup of coffee or snack meal in the rather bleak cafeteria.

It was Kate who had launched Sallie on her present adventure. 'Look, why not give the thesis a break for a few months? Why not do something totally and utterly different?'

Kate was taller than Sallie, bigger, more self-confident in every way. She had a reddish face, almost the complexion of a farmer's wife, and dark, slightly oily hair. She wore her clothes – frayed blue jeans, a black turtleneck, black leather bomber jacket – with a certain flair, which Sallie would have liked to emulate.

Sallie's hair, a mousey brown, was worn in a ponytail held by elastic bands. She wore an off-white fleece top emblazoned with a motif of teddy bears, who themselves wore red ribbons round their necks and had blue paws. She had a brown canvas skirt. Her very clean black-and-white Pumas looked tiny beside Kate's black loafers. They were tiny indeed, size ones.

The notion of doing something completely different was certainly an attractive one, though it had come as a great shock, a real blow to her self-esteem, when Kate had cheerfully said, 'Getting a job's a great way to get to know England. You know, when I first came, the first few months I was so homesick. So lonely. I just quit research for the summer and became a nanny.'

'A nanny! I've worked four years at Shaker for my BA, two at Carver for my MA! I win a scholarship to come to UCL and the best you can come up with is for me to throw it all in and start changing diapers?'

'Chris and Penny are friends of mine now and the kids are great. It's like having a new family of my own, right here in London? I just worked for them till they got a proper nanny. Then I went back to my dissertation and a whole lot of ideas I didn't even know I was working through, during that summer with the kids, had fallen into place. My mind was clear, and I just sat down and wrote, bringing in all kinds of stuff I'd read in Hélène Cixous, Hannah Arendt, that I didn't remember I'd remembered. That freed me up for my big chapter on Simone . . .'

'Weil? De Beauvoir?'

'Nina. I'm doing theories of justice as tested by some of the classic feminist texts and as reflected in popular culture? The images of women, and women's opportunities, potentialities, as reflected in . . .'

They had fallen into thesis talk, as they usually did when they met, that necessary outpouring of the lonely scholar. You read so much and had so little opportunity to discuss it. The reading experience is being fed into a mind that is always changing, for the twenty-something mind is changing as rapidly as, a decade before, the body changed. So Kate and she had parted in the BL cafeteria and no more that day had been said about nanny work.

The matter cropped up again at another of their coffee sessions and Sallie once again felt insulted by the idea, but sufficiently beguiled to note down the fact that her friend had gained her happy employment, and formed her friendship with a surrogate family, by applying to an ad in a magazine called *The Lady*. This was a magazine full of anodyne articles about gardens, topography and family life, whose small ads contained a weekly abundance of opportunity for anyone prepared to undertake domestic service, whether as part of that shrinking breed who know how to cook or serve meals, or of that much larger army of those prepared to look after other people's children while they themselves go to higher paid or more entertaining occupations, which take them out of the house.

Insulted as she was by Kate's suggestion, Sallie could not help, from the first, making stories about it inside her head; imagining herself as an adopted elder sister in some gentle family, sitting at meals with the father and mother, playing with undemanding little children by day, and continuing with Henry James and the thesis by night in her cosy bedroom in a house a bit larger and a lot warmer than Professor Helstone's.

Also, insulting as it was to think of herself as a mere babysitter, she thought of the financial security that would follow if she gave up paying rent for the bedsit in Hackney and had free accommodation with the family, in addition to her pay as a nanny.

Just how much this pay was she was staggered to discover. She had made some surreptitious enquiries, by ringing nanny agencies and pretending that she wanted to engage a young woman to look after some children. In England, they paid nannies more than they paid assistant professors!

On impulse, Sallie had applied for one of the jobs ('Start as soon as possible') advertised in that week's *The Lady*. The interview had been with a female stockbroker, living in west London. The baby screamed and spewed for the entire half-hour of the interview, while his four-year-old sister hid behind the sofa. The broker herself had hard, unsympathetic features and one of those polite English accents which really freaked Sallie. It was so cold, so very cold. As such jobs go, it was a very good one. She was offered her own bedroom, far larger than the one she occupied in Hackney, the exclusive use of a bathroom, a colour television and the negotiable use of a small car.

The woman had been desperate and that had given Sallie some satisfaction. She had said Sallie could start work at once, or delay matters for a week, if she chose. There had been a certain bluntness in Sallie's saying, there and then, that she did not think the post would suit her.

There must have been a catch, some hidden thing about this woman, or her children, which to the practised eye of a trained nanny would have been immediately obvious. *Maybe, with kids, there was always a catch.* Kids *were* the catch. Just for a moment, during that interview, Sallie had remembered the only time she had actually tried to look after a kid. She remembered the reality of it and what a disaster it had been. That interview was a warning bell. Get out of this now. Stop it. *Don't have a repetition of what happened with Jakie Kenner.*

The human brain plays funny tricks on us. That, boiled down, was the nub of what she had been trying to write about in her doctoral dissertation; and that, surely, was one of the main things that concerned her old friend Henry James.

For some reason, the very negative thoughts she had during that interview with the rich stockbroker woman in Kensington did not remain with her. She forgot her absolute disgust at the baby and her immediate loathing of the little girl, thinking she was so cute hiding behind the sofa. She forgot that she despised the woman for not looking after her own children, and she forgot how much she envied and hated her for being rich enough to pay someone else to shovel her baby's shit. The thoughts just did not stay with her.

She allowed a full two weeks to pass without giving a thought to nannying work and without picking up a copy of *The Lady*. She had returned to the library with her laptop and continued work on the thesis. It was slow work; she felt no sense of inspiration, and from time to time her interest in the subject flagged and she felt she would be happy if she never read another word of Henry James.

She went on being lonely, though, and feeling poor. One of her teeth needed fixing, and when she went to the dentist recommended by Kate, she had to write a cheque for £400.

'You never told me dentists here are as expensive as in America!'

'Some are, some aren't.' Kate smirked, tossing back her thick brown hair. 'Maybe you should think about that advice I gave you.'

Sallie did not want to tell Kate that she had already checked out the idea. To admit it, and to recall the feelings she had during that first interview, would somehow be to allow Kate to patronise her. Patronage already was a large element in their friendship; and if she was honest, this was one of the things about it which Sallie found reassuring. She liked to be bossed around. In some moods, she felt she would simply like someone to take over her life and tell her how to live it. Another bit of herself resented anyone seeing this too clearly.

'I'll think about it.' She shrugged. Then, with the sort of irony which the Group, back in Carver, made their hallmark, she said, 'Some might consider it a little *odd*, given the nature of my dissertation, that I should be thinking of working with children.'

Kate, her head full of Rawls and Arendt, had not had

time to read much James and, in fact, beyond seeing a movie of *The Wings of the Dove*, had not actually read any. The implications of the joke had been lost on her; Sallie had seen that. But when the conversation was over, and Kate had strolled back to the reading room, Sallie went out into the street, found a newsagent and began leafing through that week's *The Lady*.

She knew she was not equipped psychologically to look after babies. The memory of the Kensington interview had not faded so completely that she had forgotten the skeins of moist snot coming out of that baby's mouth and nose, and the noise it made as it squawked and grabbed and gesticulated selfishly, 'Me, me, me!' Two days of that and she'd . . . it did not bear contemplating what she might do. She would not much fancy the cutesy behind the sofa either. If, however, the magazine were to contain an ad for someone to look after older children . . . Preferably older children who had no mother hanging around in the background, patronising her, looking down on her because she needed the money, filling her with envy and hate every time she wafted out of the front door to a well-paid job or an interesting social life . . . Provided she did not have to put up with that, maybe there would be some job that would suit her.

Back home in Carver, the ironical jokes of the Group had grown as tired as old celery before she left, that she was herself a James heroine, about to take part in some emotional adventure in Europe. Milt, Ros, Heinz, Starl, Judy, they were all at it, busy reading, or rereading James or more likely flicking through the Norton Companion for the plot summaries, and ribbing Sallie as the new Kate Croy, ready to con a sick heiress out of her fortune, or Charlotte Stant cunningly looking to find a way of holding on to her prince, while deceiving her best friend.

What would the Group, then, have made of this? The advertisement stared from the small ads as if it were printed in bold. Two children, eight and ten, living in the country needed 'a nanny-friend. No domestic duties (full-time housekeeper employed) but full responsibility required, since without parents. Apply to a telephone number.'

The ad itself was a short story, a mystery sufficiently Jamesian. And she had, from the very beginning, the strange, not to say uncanny, sense that she was walking into her own thesis subject, that she was becoming the central figure in that story which she had been so obsessively contemplating all year.

She had gone back to the library and immediately, before returning to the reading room, had rung the number indicated. A secretary had answered, but when Sallie announced her business she had been put through almost directly.

The voice – his voice – Charles's voice – the voice of the man she knew almost from the first that she was going to love – was the male equivalent of that terrible cold voice of the Kensington woman stockbroker. Whereas the female version made you feel put down, it sneered at you from a height, the male version, honeyed and aristocratic, was quite literally seductive. It made you think Mr Rochester and Max de Winter. It made you think danger, big houses catching fire, eternal passion shrieked through night winds.

'Ideally, of course, I am looking for someone who wants a permanent position . . . But, naturally . . . No, I am grateful to you for being so candid . . . No, no, much better to make it clear at the outset . . . Even a few weeks would help . . . It is the school holidays which pose the real . . . Miles is still away at . . .'

'Excuse me?'

'Michael, that's my son, is still away at his boarding school but he will be back . . .'

She could have sworn that he said his son was called Miles. She had been on the verge of explaining the extraordinary coincidence, that Miles is the name of the little boy in Henry James's story, the story where a young woman is asked to go down to . . .

But now he was speaking of his house and its situation. 'I have to say that Staverton is not everyone's cup of tea. I'll be completely candid, there have been girls, young women, er . . . young ladies, who have been down and taken one look at the place . . . It is, you see, very remote. There's nothing like a nightlife.'

'I can do without clubs for a week or two.'

'I'm sorry?'

Her joke, for such it had been, did not seem so funny when repeated.

'Flora goes to school nearby, a day school, so part of your job would be to take and fetch. But her term ends soon and then you'd be her – well, her companion.'

'So Flora's how old?'

'Frances – my daughter is called Frances. She is eight. Mike's ten. They're great, very easy . . . It's my great regret in life that I can't see more of them. They need a father in the circumstances, which – well, if you are serious about this job, I can explain the circumstances . . .'

So the appointment for an interview had been made. She was to present herself the next day. 'Ten, ten fifteen – make it ten fifteen, but come early in case I can see you earlier. I'm interviewing counsel at eleven, and it's an important case. It might, unfortunately, take me to Hong Kong, but I can explain that when we meet . . . Super! . . . Look forward to it . . . er, Sallie. Goodbye.'

The next twenty hours, only a few of which could be eliminated by sleep, had been largely devoted to the difficult question of what, in her limited wardrobe, to wear. Most of the clothes in her closet in Hackney had been taken out, shaken, put on, surveyed in front of the mirror and taken off again. She decided against make-up, knowing that when she wore it, it made her look like a child who'd been playing with her mother's lipstick. Then she put on some lipstick to make sure and, having made sure, wiped it off again.

It was a pity she was so pallid. She feared that blusher would have a circus-clown effect, but the even pallor of her cheeks, brow and lips might not impress a man whose house was six miles from the nearest railroad station and who had asked if she could ride. A more outdoor complexion would have reassured him perhaps? The red sweater made her look even paler and the stripy rainbow sweater had not been washed recently enough. Though it did not stink too obviously, there was a whiff of armpits as she pulled it over her head. The brown pants suit she'd worn for lunch with the Helstones looked like, and was, borrowed from her mom; and surely the last thing she needed to look, if applying for this job, was middle-aged?

In the end, she travelled eastwards at the appointed hour in her daily outfit of tiny clean Pumas, brown canvas skirt, ribbed grey sweater and fleece top covered with teddy bears. She had showered and washed her hair, but having tried various other ways of brushing it, she knew she felt safer with a ponytail, even if it did look a little childish.

'I am a child' – the thought formed quite articulately in her head – 'compared with *him*.'

Chapter Two

Emerging an hour later into the watercolour sunshine of Bishopsgate, her pale face had a love story written all over it. Her eyes sparkled, her cheeks were pink. She could barely contain her feelings of exaltation. She wanted to dance down the street.

There was no wife!

'I'm afraid the children have no mother . . .'

'Oh, I'm so sorry', she had lied. 'And when . . .'

'We've all been alone, oh, nearly two years now.'

'That's just so awful . . .'

'We manage. You have to, don't you?'

So, he was a widower, aged . . . oh, what the hell did age matter when a man looked like Lord Byron?

She was used to mixing with her exact coevals and found it difficult to judge the ages of those older. Forty, was he? Less. If he was thirty-five, that made him only eight years older than her!

She had sensed immediately that it was hurt which kept him away from Staverton. 'I'm busy – ridiculously busy, as it happens,' he had said. 'And the big cases always seem to crop up when I'd rather be with the children . . .'

When he had said that, she had felt him, as it were, reaching out for her, needing her.

'Staverton's a place . . . as you can guess . . . which has its unhappy associations . . .'

Had he said that? Or had she just made him say it in the rerun of the conversation that had been playing inside her head since she came down in the glass elevator and skipped out on to the sidewalk?

'Let me lay my cards on the table and be absolutely frank with you, Sallie.'

Those words he had quite definitely said. She had been sitting in the swivel chair opposite his neat desk. He was on the other side of the desk, his crinkly dark-brown hair resting against the high leather chairback. Behind the chair was a plate-glass window, a bright blue sky, a modern cityscape abutting something much older. Beyond a glass block a steeple, which she felt might be one of the famous ones, caught the bright March light.

On the clean blotter, between two neatly piled sets of documents, he put his hands together, as if in prayer. He had long, strong fingers with very clean nails. No ring – was that a signal to her?

'The children are without their mother, obviously. That's been made clear to you?'

'I'm just so, so sorry . . .' she had begun, but he had not allowed her to continue.

In his sharp, intelligent and very dark-blue eyes, in his slightly upturned nose and chiselled features, there was something so playful, so boyish, and at the same time so sad.

'These things happen,' he said. 'Look. There is an excellent housekeeper down at Staverton, Gloria, and in the absence of a proper nanny in the last term, she has been looking after the children – looking after Frances, at any rate. Michael has been away at school for much of the time. But Gloria is married, she has a lot on her plate and she very understandably needs to go home to her long-suffering husband. I can't go on exploiting her good nature. I was going to take the children to Cornwall next week, but they've changed the date of the court hearing in Hong Kong and I simply have to go abroad. Also – this is just the way things pan out when you are in a fix' – he looked at her entirely without self-pity and smiled – 'we had a perfectly good nanny lined up to stay with the children for three weeks and she has now let us down.'

He looked at his fingernails.

'Look. This is to throw you in at the deep end. You haven't met the children and what we are saying, that they need . . .' he looked up with such a strange expression on his face. She had seen such *need* there '. . . is a mother, frankly. Which is *not* – you understand . . .'

She had nodded vigorously, to show that she more than understood.

He was auditioning her, not for the role of temporary nanny, but of . . . the kids' mother! She knew it sounded crazy to be having these thoughts so soon; she knew that he had not said, in so many words, that what he wanted was her to move in, with him and his children, on a permanent basis. But some words did not need to be said.

Pirouetting towards the plate-glass door of a coffee shop, one of those big multinational places she and the Group vowed they'd never, ever patronise, she bought herself a cardboard cup of latte, wriggled on to a high stool and watched the City workers pass to and fro on the sidewalk outside. They were much better turned out than the ragbag of individuals you saw drifting up and down the Euston Road between the library and her old Hall of Residence in Mabledon Place. The men wore dark suits and silk ties. The women, with nice hairdos, careful make-up, bags and shoes of the kind photographed in magazines, expensive clothes, could have been in Indianapolis or even Chicago. Sallie felt that her own outfit, which was just fine for having a coffee in the library, was painfully unstylish; and the teddy bears on the fleece top, for the first time since she had bought the garment, seemed inappropriate.

Yet he hadn't minded that she was dressed in this way. Frankly, he was a bit less petty than that. Also, he saw through to the real Sallie. That sensual, curved mouth of his, and that nose, they were the features of some Regency fantasy. Bursting, almost spluttering, with her happiness, almost laughing aloud with it, she was saying inside her head, 'Excuse me, but forget Mr Rochester. We are into serious, serious Mr Darcy territory here.'

And then again, he was so funny. He had a wonderfully dry wit.

'Before you give me an answer, I had better tell you a little about me, a little about Staverton. It may strike you as a rum set-up'.

Rum! *Delicious.*

'Don't let it scare you,' he said. She had felt him almost undressing her as he said it.

'Gloria is the housekeeper and, without her, frankly, I don't know where I'd have been in the last couple of years.'

Sallie felt instantaneous dislike of Gloria for that, while telling herself not to be so ridiculous. Gloria was a servant; he had never asked Gloria, within minutes of meeting her, to stand in for his children's mother.

'I don't want to go into all the details – but you can imagine they are painful. The reason I keep the children down at Staverton and not at the flat in London is – partly because they are country animals and partly because they do need to be . . . protected. You understand that? They do need supervising – more than most kids of their age. I want someone with them at all times, is that clear?'

This was very far from clear.

'In London, one holidays, they went missing. You can imagine the nightmare. Kidnap is a melodramatic word, but what else was it? They came back – else we shouldn't be having this conversation – but I don't want to go down that road again and frankly, while I am abroad . . .'

He pressed the perfectly clean blotter very hard with his long clean hands. It was a gesture of firmness, even of anger.

None of this made sense, exactly, but she did not have the courage to ask him to spell out what he meant. He seemed to be under the impression, either that someone else had explained to her the set-up at Staverton, or that he had already done so during their telephone conversation.

'Whoever does this job is going to have a pretty heavy burden of responsibility. She'll be sleeping in the house alone with the children. She won't have to cook or clean or shop, but she will be in sole charge of the children. You understand that?'

'Of course.'

'As I said to you on the telephone, I was really looking for someone who would be full-time and stay a year or so. In the light of the fact that the agency nanny has let us down so badly at the last minute there might, frankly, be a case for employing someone such as yourself who is only available for a month or two. After that . . .'

He had lifted the palms from the blotter and spread them wide, like wings. Then he had put the hands behind his curly head, looked at her and laughed. 'So, Sallie! Over to you! Tell me about yourself.'

The résumé, the actual printout, had been produced and passed across the desk as she fumblingly repeated, as if they were her own words, sentences said to her in the cafeteria by Kate.

'There comes a moment in an academic life when maybe the brain needs a little rest, when . . .'

'And I see you have worked with children before?'

He had looked at her quite searchingly at that moment. Into the regular résumé that she kept in her documents file, she had added a sentence or two about looking after the Kenner brat that sad summer she was stuck in Muncie and needed money badly.

Her nondescript replies had made him lean forward and smile at her, not threateningly, but almost conspiratorially, as if they were sharing a joke at the Kenners' expense. 'You survived? The kid survived?'

'Just!'

They had laughed to ease the tension.

'Obviously, if you are prepared to take this job, I want you to start at once. But if you could give me a reference or two?'

'Maybe Professor Helstone – my supervisor?'

'He's in London?'

'Yup.'

'So' – and Charles had produced from the inside pocket of his dark-grey suit jacket a gold fountain pen. Slowly, he had unscrewed the cap and, preparing to write on a very clean, white piece of paper, he said, 'Fire ahead. If I could take his name as a reference – and an e-mail, perhaps? Or a telephone number?'

She rummaged in the brown Trunk-co knapsack at her knees, which looked, in the setting of that palatial office, just a little unsophisticated. A small pocket diary

contained the professor's private line in his teaching room
off Gower.

'And – just in case. If you had a telephone number for . . .'

'My mom?'

'No, what is the name of the family? The American
family?'

She had been appalled at the prospect of him telephoning
her mother.

The worst case would be him calling up Mrs Kenner by
phone and having his mind poisoned against Sallie. Maybe
it would have been better to invent a family where she'd
worked as nanny. If challenged, she could always say they'd
moved on, lost touch, in the way people do. As it was, in
the tense panic of the interview she had had to think fast,
and she knew that had any member of the Group been in
a similar situation she would have been perfectly prepared
to lie for them.

She had decided quickly to nominate her friend Lorrie
as the person who could most plausibly impersonate Mrs
Kenner, should Charles Masters choose to take up the
reference. A quick e-mail would put Lorrie in the picture.
All she needed to do (*if* he called her – and he'd probably
be too busy) was to say that Sallie had worked for her kid
in Muncie during the summer four years ago, that everything had been fine, bla, bla, bla. Five minutes would fix
it. Sallie would have done the same for Lorrie.

She dictated Lorrie's telephone number.

'That's the city code for Muncie?' he asked sharply, when
she had said the first three numbers.

'I guess so,' she'd said, a little unconvincingly, since she
had already stated that her mother lived in, that she herself
in some senses came from, Muncie.

'Right,' he said, as the numbers, neat and wet in their

black ink, glistened reproachfully as blood on the paper.

'Now – as I say, I had been meaning to take the children down to Cornwall in a few days. That will have to be postponed until I return from Hong Kong. We are in an emergency. Could you, do you think, go down to Staverton provisionally for three weeks – a month? I'll be back from Hong Kong by then. You'd be doing us all a very great favour.'

That was how he had chosen to put it. She should do this thing *for him*. Though she would not actually be with him, she was going to his house almost as a trial bride. 'Tell me a bit about your work – your academic work,' he had said politely. There had been nothing so vulgar as hurry in his manner as he had made the enquiry, but he had not been able to refrain from lifting the crisp white shirt cuff, the gold cuff-link, the charcoal-grey cuff with its four bone buttons to consult the Rolex. He had done it surreptitiously, but she had felt it was a signal that she should keep her reflections on Henry James as short as possible.

It was flattering, but also just a little scary, that he turned out to know something about her subject. Maybe, he'd been a literature major before turning to the law. He asked her if she knew – his manner implied, *But, of course you do!* – who had first told Henry James the anecdote on which his novella was based. Professor Helstone had been talking about this during one of their supervisions and she had tried, as politely as possible, to suggest that she was hoping to shy away from such anecdotal, historicist approaches. Her concern was to be with structures, with narrative voices, with the critical history of the text and the ways in which it had been treated since the postmodern revolution in theory. Foucault, Todorov and Roland Barthes were more germane to her purposes than the unheard-of churchman whose name Helstone had asked her to consider. Now, she heard it again and felt rather differently about it, as Charles Masters came out with – 'Archbishop Benson!'

'Excuse me?'

'I remember being told that by an old great-aunt who was a sort of cousin of the Bensons. I suppose that makes me a cousin too. Aunt Sybil, bless her, always maintained that Staverton was the house in the story, but I think that is rather far-fetched. It certainly was the Archbishop of Canterbury who first told James the story. It is there in his notebooks. Well, you know all this much better than I do. What do you think of the opera?'

It felt pathetic – in honesty, she knew it was pathetic – to reply that not merely had she never been to the opera, but that she had never even played the CD to herself. 'I'm afraid I . . .'

'Don't care for Britten? There are purists who don't. You must be one. I wonder if I can persuade you one day to change your mind.'

My God, he had known her twenty-five minutes and he was wanting to take her to the opera.

'I saw it at Covent Garden a few years ago' – he peered at her to see if he was making sense. He was too much of a gentleman actually to explain what Covent Garden was. It felt like something in the nature of a trick question. 'Of course when you are there, it is a sense of occasion . . . You see all these fat cats sitting around who've block-booked tickets, and have no interest in music and just want to crowd into the bar for champagne in the interval. But the night we saw it – my wife was still . . . It held them – even the corporate entertainers. The children, so completely fixated on the ghosts – the ghosts speak, or rather sing, in the opera, of course, which they don't as I recollect in the story.'

Beyond hearing snatches on the radio, Sallie had never actually attended any opera and she wondered, when she confessed this, whether he would find it charming or the opposite. Today was obviously not the moment for such a confession.

'The sheer terror of it – the situation!' he was saying, his face for a moment changed by the awfulness of James's ghost story. 'You really did feel the children being sucked into evil. But – arrangements.' He tapped the blotter impatiently. 'If I ring Gloria, she can meet you off a train tomorrow – say, late morning? It is an hour and a half from Charing Cross. I'm afraid you will find Staverton very cut off – it is six miles from the nearest station and two or three miles from anything much in the way of a village. People assume the south-east of England is completely over-built and overcrowded, which it is, but there are still pockets of remoteness, even in Kent. My secretary will give you the train details.'

Once again, the sleeve had been lifted and a surreptitious glance at the gold watch had been made. This time, she had known this heralded the end of the interview.

As he led her to the door, 'Maybe,' she'd said, 'I'll go and buy the CD – play it on my Discman.'

'Oh, do! I'd be fascinated to know what you think. Myfanwy Piper wrote the libretto, of course.'

Why of course? And who was Myfanwy Piper? Was this, like Archbishop Benson, another cousin?

'And it has the same title as the story, right? The opera?'

'Oh, yes,' he said cheerily. He showed her into the elevator and, as the doors swooshed shut, he was confirming, '*The Turn of the Screw.*'

Chapter Three

She watched England judder and flit past the smudged train window: the sweep of the great river with, on one side of it, the familiar landmark of the Houses of Parliament, on the other a great power station, vaguely Babylonian in its scorched orange brick. Then mile on mile of back gardens followed, the self-contained lives of these people she would never know, wet clothes pegged out on devices resembling umbrellas blown wrong way out; cats hunched on stock-brick walls; ragstone churches she would never visit; and at every station more and more faces, many of them, until the outer suburbs were cleared, black. The whole thing a mystery, a puzzle book with no solutions offered at the back.

She had bought the *International Herald Tribune* at the railroad station. Maybe it would have been better to try an English newspaper, but whenever she had made the effort before, the experiment had not yielded much. It could have been in a different language for all the sense she could make of the arch jokes, and the preoccupation with politicians, TV stars and minor celebrities of whom she had never heard. Back home, they had cryptic crosswords; here, they had cryptic newspapers, with only the stuff about the Royal Family being either intelligible or interesting. Then, last time she'd tried one of the English newspapers, her eye had lighted on this truly horrifying article (meant to be funny), which expressed not merely an understandable political distrust of the United States, but a true hatred of Americans. It mocked their clothes, the way they spoke, the way they moved. It claimed that they were too obese to 'waddle' (this was the author's word) up Oxford Street. The rancour of the piece was appalling, forcing the fear that simply by opening her mouth and speaking, Sallie was setting up a comparable set of responses. Was this what they all, secretly, thought of Americans but were too polite to say?

She felt safer with the dear, dry old *Tribune* with its synopses of world events, its intelligent articles, which did not try to be too clever. Rather, they were clever enough, but they did not try to be, in a useful expression she had first heard on the lips of Professor Helstone, 'too clever by half'. (He'd been discussing one of the modern theorists.)

As she snuggled comfortably, as beneath a blanket, into an article about the democratic primaries, the suburbs outside the window at last gave place to rolling fields, to grazing Friesians, and oaks and sycamores just bursting into leaf. In fields where sun shone faintly, horse-chestnuts had come into bright-green leaf. They were ready to trumpet their blossoms.

Red brick changed to old stone, brown sandstone, flint. There was an atmosphere, though no sight, of the sea, something in the slight mistiness wafting on field and village. Churches, when passed, were now noticeably older. Shingled spires and turreted towers peeped from clumps of old trees, at odds with the zooming highways, the warehouses, the pylons, the out-of-town malls.

She had been informed that the journey to Lymingbourne takes one hour and twenty minutes. At this station she was to get out and Gloria would be expecting her.

To say that she felt nervous was an understatement. London had scared and depressed her equally, but it had not fenced her in. She came and went from the bedsit in Raymond Road quite freely. She went to bed, got up, when she liked. She clocked into the library when it suited her.

That morning, her last in London for a few weeks, perhaps longer, a rush of doubts had overcome her. This was *running away*. She hadn't given London a chance. She had not given any of it, her life in the Hall of Residence, a chance. Would it not have been open to her to go out and meet a few people? Could she not have started to attend a church, joined one of the many graduate societies, signed on for a language class? Pilates or yoga? Overtures from fellow grads in the Hall of Residence – Grant, Zoe, Janie – had never been followed up. Even with the few Americans she had sort-of befriended, such as Kate, she had been too much the passive partner. Had she ever been the one to initiate things with Kate – suggest going for a meal or a movie? Could she not have waited until the others in her Hackney household had returned from Tunisia and maybe suggested that one night a week they all ate together? What was she now doing, letting herself be taken to a place where she was six miles from the nearest train station and where she knew nobody, nobody at all?

Yesterday, at one p.m., as soon as it had been breakfast time in Muncie, she had phoned her mother, who had been perhaps still a little woozy with Valium.

'Are you crazy? After what happened last time, you're going to work with kids? Sallie, don't do it!'

'Mom, it's a temporary job, it's maybe three, four weeks at *most*. And Charles Masters is *not* Mrs Kenner.'

'Maybe not, but he's going to want to check you out, right? He's going to need references – he'll call up Mrs Kenner and then the whole thing will come out.'

'Mom – it *won't* come out.'

'You think Mrs Kenner won't tell him what happened with Jakie in the bathtub? You're crazy.'

'Mom, don't keep saying I'm crazy.'

Her mother had come out with a whole load of stuff about the Kenners, which she just did not want to hear. During that nightmare summer four years ago, the summer Sallie had been their babysitter, the Kenners had been going through a bad patch in their marriage. They had subsequently sorted this out. They'd gotten divorced. Jakie would be, how time flew, eleven by now.

Her mother had begun to bang on about how well she had always felt herself regarded by the neighbours until the incident, little chats with Mrs Kenner if they met out in the street or down the Cash and Carry; how Mrs Kenner would always ask about how Sal was getting along at college and how Mom had always taken an interest in little Jakie, how she'd been the one who first suggested that Sal work for Mrs Kenner, give her some time off that summer to get herself organised while she tried to get back to work as an oral hygienist, how Mrs Kenner hadn't felt the need to check Sallie out – the Declans and the Kenners were friends. Were. Had been.

'Mom, it was an *accident*!' Sallie had shouted this into the receiver. She felt really let down by her mother in this. Her edginess was increased by the fact that Lorrie had e-mailed, at some length, to express unhappiness about impersonating Mrs Kenner, should Charles Masters call her number. She had felt, Lorrie, that the least Sallie could do was to explain to her why she could not use Mrs Kenner as a reference. Was Jakie the boy, Lorrie jocularly enquired, whom Sallie once boasted she'd nearly murdered? Sallie's accounts of the incident, and the subsequent fights with the Kenners, had been swathed in ambiguities, which Lorrie felt to be unfair.

Why could neither Lorrie nor Sallie's mom see that the incident in the bathroom with Jakie had nothing to do with her present little vacation job in Kent? The idea that the incident would repeat itself with Miles and Flora was simply ridiculous. Sallie Declan was not a child batterer. She was not mentally disturbed. The way Mom and Lorrie spoke, you would guess she had been both. All Lorrie need say, if Charles Masters phoned, was that Sallie had been a great babysitter, that her kid loved having her look after him, end of story. All her mom had needed to say, on the phone, was she hoped her daughter would be happy in the post and not too lonesome stuck in the middle of the English countryside. Sallie had neither sought nor expected the judgemental tone that both women had used; all she'd needed from them was support. There were quite enough other people in the world prepared to do her down. From a friend and from a mother, a girl was entitled to a little friendship and a little motherliness.

Look, all that happened was, for a split second, she had lost control. That happens to anyone dealing with kids.

Sallie Declan was a perfectly responsible person. There had been no need, absolutely no need, in the course of a twenty-minute interview, to start telling Charles Masters about the prescription drugs she'd been taking since high school, anyway since Shaker Oakes. There was no need for her to empty her purse and show him the cartons of her present antidepressant. And when Lorrie e-mailed to say that Sallie should have told him about Jakie Kenner, did she really suppose he'd've given her a job after that?

'I think that covers things,' he had said. 'Unless there is anything you feel you want to say at this point?'

Lorrie thought, did she, that this would have been a good moment to say, 'Yeah, the last kid I looked after was taken to hospital by paramedics, sirens wailing, lights flashing, blood all over the bathroom wall'?

While he was sneaking a look at the Rolex on his beautiful wrist, was that what Charles Masters had needed to hear?

Sallie still considered herself a perfectly responsible person. It seemed to have slipped the minds both of her mother and of Lorrie that the incident happened more than four years ago.

A man came to check her ticket. She still wasn't used to this, having travelled so seldom on trains here. The constant mistrust was insulting, almost a threat. Back home, you paid your money, you stuck your Amtrak ticket in the slot over your head and away you went. There was not all this rummaging, peering, prying.

'How much further to Bly?'

'Where's that, my love?'

She smiled at the familiarity. 'Excuse me, Lymingbourne?'

'In about twenty minutes, love.'

She leaned back against the headrest, parsing and repunctuating the sentence she had just heard.

In about twenty minutes. Love. It had come in about twenty minutes, rather less. Charles Masters's chin was

31

deeply cleft. How did he manage to shave each morning without the razor blade slicing those beautifully chiselled indentations? His dark eyes had looked straight into hers. They had seen her heart. Twenty minutes love.

'Well, of course, what they need is' – he had said it with such a sad little smile – 'a mother'.

The kids, he meant. They needed a mother. In twenty minutes, had he found one? What is a mother? A lady married to the kids' father. They need a mother. What does that mean, if not, I need a wife. Will you be their mother? What did that mean, if not . . . ? Can she have been hearing right? Within twenty minutes he had been proposing marriage to her without actually using the words.

Stranger things have happened. Mrs Sallie Declan Masters. Of Staverton, in Kent.

'Have *you* checked *him* out?' Mom had changed tack. 'How did his wife die – you did say she was dead, didn't you? Why couldn't he get a divorce like normal folks? What happens if you find yourself walled up in some big house in the middle of nowhere and he's some kind of maniac? What happens if there aren't any kids at all – have you thought of that?'

Mom had started on a rambling, completely illogical recollection of some article she'd read in the *Inquirer* about women in Europe being lured into white slavery by gangs of Albanians.

Sallie's worries were other, quite other. She did seriously hope that the children would like her. So much, already, hung on this. It would be simply awful if, having begun so well with the father, she should find that the ungrateful little creatures rejected her, perhaps for the very reason that their father regarded her so highly.

What if, once again, she found herself confronted with

a child who was simply impossible? A child who would not do what it was told? A child who sought to undermine her, to humiliate her?

For a moment, her hazel, slightly cloudy eyes could focus neither upon the view from the window nor upon the newspaper. She could see Jakie Kenner, aged seven, sitting in the bathtub and saying, quite calmly, 'Know somethin', Sal? You're a fat asshole . . . You, Sallie Declan are one fat asshole. Your butt is . . .'

The sheer impudence on the child's face as he had said the words had come like a physical blow. The sentences had been uttered after days of failure, days in which she had tried everything to amuse him, days in which she had cooked for him, ridden a bike with him, taken him to the park, days in which he had refused to be her friend, refused to speak to her, days in which he'd asked, no sooner than she'd started some boring game with him, to be allowed to play computer games on his own in peace, days in which he'd been cheeky, naughty, downright hateful. It wasn't right that a child should be allowed to say such sentences as he was now so calmly enunciating as he sat in his bathwater.

'Your butt is . . .'

She would not let him say anything about her butt. He must have fallen against the faucet. That's what she had kept saying afterwards, to herself, and to anyone who'd listen. What she didn't say was that he'd fallen because she'd hit him. It had been a severe blow, against the side of the head, which sent it ricocheting like a punchball against the sharp faucet. There was blood pouring from the side of his head, blood which changed the bathwater to red in seconds, blood all over the floor, as she grabbed at him, lifted him, blood all over her, mopping ineffectually with a white towel soon turning scarlet.

He should never have said those words. Of course she could not repeat them to anyone, though he had done so, when he recovered; told his mother a garbled version of the whole thing. At first there had just been the nightmare of his limp body, which anger made her suppose to be faking unconsciousness. As she'd shaken it, more blood had spurted, some spattering the mirror and walls. An ambulance had been summoned. Mrs Kenner had appeared, eventually, at the hospital. The doctors and paramedics had asked questions, questions, questions, but when Mrs Kenner came, they had decided, the police did not need to be brought in. It had been an accident.

Later that evening, a telephone call from Mr Kenner had calmly informed her that she would not be needed to babysit next day. Jakie was fine. Concussed, but fine. They did not want her back, looking after their kid.

Jakie Kenner was a little scumbag. He was the pits. She would never know, exactly, what he'd told his mother, but it was obviously the most ridiculous exaggeration. Flora and Miles were going to be something very different. They were not Mrs Kenner's kids, for a start. They were the children of Charles Masters. And what they needed was a mother.

Chapter Four

'You're Sallie.'

'Is it so obvious?'

'Since you ask . . .'

She had lugged the vast tortoiseshell of a backpack up on to her shoulders, while one fist held a laptop in its plastic case, the other the faithful brown knapsack. The tall blonde woman who stood before her, obviously Gloria, stretched out an arm.

'I'd shake hands if I could,' said Sallie.

'Here, I'll take some of that off you – phew, what have you got in here? Bricks?'

'Some books.'

'I could have saved you the trouble – there are more than enough books at Staverton.'

Strength and height were the two qualities of Gloria that were instantaneously striking. She was a good six inches taller than Sallie. Her big hand, slightly rough, enfolded Sallie's when she shook it. She had dyed blonde hair, cut by a hairdresser somewhat severely. On a bulky frame, she wore a dark-blue sweater. Black, sporty trousers hugged her very long legs, whose well-shaped calves were emphasised by the white stripe running down their side. She was about the age of Sallie's mother, around fifty, but in a much better state of fitness and repair. Her face, slightly shiny, was much more highly coloured than Sallie's; neither ruddy, nor suntanned, but weather-beaten. She had eyebrows but they were very faint. Her eyes were greyish blue, quite close together, and her lips were thin. Sallie thought them cruel.

'I wasn't sure what to bring so I . . .' Sallie's sentence did not end anywhere as she struggled to keep up with Gloria's healthy pace. 'In the end, better to pack too much than too little . . . Are you sure you don't mind carrying that bag?'

Taking no notice of these apologetic utterances, Gloria said, 'This is us,' and indicated a Japanese jeep in the station parking lot.

'That certainly weighs a ton,' said Gloria, as she helped Sallie shrug and shuffle with her huge framed backpack.

'I didn't reckon you'd have these particular books – they're ones I need for my college work,' she explained.

'Oh, yeah? You're still studying, then?' Gloria did not appear to be impressed.

'And here you see the fleshpots of Lymingbourne.'

By the time Sallie had turned her slightly cricked shoulder in order to get a better view of a winding high street, a large eighteenth-century building with brick arcades beneath a parade of old Georgian houses, some modern shopfronts, a tall church with a spire, a fish and chip shop and a place to fix new exhaust pipes, the Honda had swung past amber traffic lights and sped on to the open road out of town.

They drove up a mile of highway, took a left down a narrow road between thick hedges and swooped downwards into a wooded coomb. Gloria drove masterfully, talking as she commanded steering wheel and gear handle. You'll find just Frances at home. Michael's still away at boarding school. They'll break up later.'

Back home it was marriages which broke up. Here the kids did it? 'The children don't live together?'

'The boys' term for some reason goes on longer than the girls.'

'She's not at a boarding school?'

'She's at Alice Chase,' said Gloria, making no effort to explain what this might imply. 'Michael's only started to board this last term. It's not the way I'd bring up my own children, but – in the circumstances . . .'

Gloria's large hand holding the wheel extended its fingers before clasping it more firmly.

Sallie, staring ahead at the twisting road, inwardly asked why she had taken so instant a dislike to Gloria. She lighted upon a literary explanation. Gloria was so crudely unlike Mrs Grose, the housekeeper in *The Turn of the Screw*. Sallie had wanted a homely body, not this tall, self-confident and, yes, sexy person. She realised that some of the moments in the James tale that touched her most were those when the terrified governess takes the old housckeeper into her confidence, and the two women embrace and clasp one another. Sallie had been in quest of such a figure? Was that one of her reasons, a primary reason, for accepting Charles Masters's precipitate offer? A bosom to cry on?

'I expect Charles explained the set-up?' Gloria said abrasively. 'Frannie's at home. Michael gets back at the end of the week from his school. They're decent enough kids. Give 'em a horse or a tennis racquet and they're happy. You ride?'

'That's horses, right?'

'We don't run to camels, I'm afraid,' Gloria retorted.

There had been riding lessons, a few, in the days when

her parents were still together and when her mother aspired
to a slightly grander way of life. The Saturday mornings at
the pony club had been fairly good torture, as she
recollected, and in the intervening nineteen years Sallie had
not foreseen any circumstances in which she would be
forced to get on another animal's back.

'I can ride,' she said.

'That's a relief, at any rate.' Gloria's tone implied that
Sallie's ability to ride was one small consolation in a list of
otherwise wholly undesirable personal attributes. 'The last
girl fell off. The nearest accident and emergency unit's
twelve miles away, and of course it was Buggins who had
to drive her in.'

After the ten seconds required to register the identity of
Buggins, Sallie said, 'I'll have to try to stay in the saddle!
Or maybe they can go for rides without me?'

'That's something Charles has explained? They are *never*
to be left. He told you what happened in Notting Hill?'

'Not in so many words. Notting Hill is where he lives
in London?'

'We tried the experiment of their having one of the
school holidays in London. It should have been okay – I
believe he organised a Norland nanny, the best.' A signifi-
cant pause spoke of the contrast between what the
Norland nanny could provide and the present makeshift
arrangement. 'The inevitable happened, I'm afraid.'

'The children got lost?'

Gloria sniffed and concentrated on changing gear. 'I don't
know what Charles has told you,' she said. 'It isn't for me
to tell you things, if he hasn't said anything. It's his business. All I'm saying is this isn't any ordinary job. You have
got to make sure the children are supervised. They may be
ten and eight, but the supervision has to be constant. That's

why I just couldn't go on with it on my own. Staverton's a big place – well, you'll see how big – and I'm very much a hands-on person. If I do a thing, I do it properly.'

'Of course.'

'There's always something to do at Staverton and although I love the kids – don't get me wrong – I just couldn't go on as we were going. Besides, it wasn't fair on Ken.'

Gloria drove with an air of decisive confidence. Sallie noticed such things. She was an extremely anxious driver herself – who had never got as far as taking a driving test. This was another matter which had not been fully aired during her interview with Charles Masters. She had, in fact, given him to understand that driving was not a problem.

As a passenger, she was also anxious. Already, given the swiftness and assurance with which Gloria forced the jeep to hug hedges, skim verges, accelerate up hills, Sallie began to suffer from motion sickness. It was with less than full concentration that she attended to the topographical commentary as they came to a village.

'This is Newtonards for what it's worth.'

A place sign, stuck into the sward at the side of the road, confirmed the assertion. Gloria did not seem too troubled by the request printed beneath: 'Please drive slowly through the village.'

A hand at the wheel, extending fingers towards the right-hand mirror accompanied the observation, 'Shop. Or was. The last shop we had within five miles of the house. Tesco put paid to that. Pub still stays open, though, if you like a drink . . . Church if you're into that . . . and that's us.'

She indicated a small modern bungalow, with a velvet-smooth lawn edged with the brighter spring bulbs. Sallie's heart missed a jolt. Nothing, either in Charles's description of Staverton nor in his leisured, aristocratic demeanour, had suggested a place on this modest scale. She wondered with some dismay if there was space in this little house for them all to sleep without her being asked to share a bedroom. Whose would she share? The children's? Gloria's?

'Charles is always urging us to take one of the cottages on the estate, but Ken's not having any of that. He says anything could happen. No disrespect to Charles, he works his socks off to keep the place and the last two years – well . . . poor bugger, pardon my French. But as Ken says, Charles could sell the whole estate tomorrow to some Japanese consortium and then where would *we* be?'

'That was where *you* live?'

They had whizzed past the bungalow.

'When I have the chance. You see why we're so anxious to have someone in the house sleeping over with the kids. Ken's been over to Staverton himself, of course. Charles is perfectly happy for him to do that, but you see it from Ken's point of view. He wants to sleep in his own house with his own wife.'

'Charles doesn't visit weekends?'

'It's always the idea; says he means to. There's meaning and doing, isn't there?'

'Uh-huh.'

It did not take long to roar through Newtonards.

'Ken – he's your husband, right?'

'Was when I last looked – was when I cooked his breakfast.' When her laughter ceased, Gloria added, 'No, it'll be twenty-eight years come May Day.'

'Ken doesn't work in the house, on the estate?'

'It's worked out better that he doesn't. He'll help out. Help anyone, Ken will, and both the kids love him. Kids do. Have to be good with kids in his line, little blighters. He's a good judge of their characters, too, which is part of it. He wouldn't sell to any kid who wasn't going to be responsible, look after their animal.'

'Ken is in the business of . . . ?'

'Ken runs the pet shop in Lymingbourne. Plus there's the cattery – hence the sign.'

'I missed it.'

'You *missed* it?' This was ribbing, intended to be fun, but with that edge of cruelty which always accompanies a tease. 'Sorry you missed the sign; we're rather proud of it. Ken cut it out with a fretsaw. It's just a bit of ply, but in the shape of a cat. Paint it black – he did the lettering with stencils.'

The road began to climb and wind. Gloria's foot was on the gas and Sallie felt her stomach heaving. Stage one of motion nausea, the faintly disagreeable sensations in breast and ears, had been passed. Stage two, the actual heaving of the stomach, was now well under way. It was going to take her fullest concentration to hold at bay stage three, which was the inevitable. She looked desperately at the car door and wondered which of the various handles or switches controlled the (electronically operated?) windows.

'Do you mind if we wind down the . . .'

'Stacey's Wood,' said Gloria, as they drove through a glade. Her own familiarity with the landscape was so deep that no explanations or commentary were now offered. Her tone implied that the little wood was as well known as the Bois de Boulogne. 'And this wall here's the beginning of the estate.'

Sallie's silence, as she fidgeted with the *Windows down* button, was taken by Gloria as incomprehension. She glossed, 'We're enterin' Masters country.' She spoke this in a funny voice not her own. After lurching about a bit on a rough patch of track, Sallie realised that the accent, which at first she had taken as a stab at Irish, was meant to be American.

Leaving Stacey's Wood behind them, the jeep nosed into a narrow road between two low-built red-brick walls which ended in a hamlet: a medieval church, St Peter in Chains – some heavy yew trees and a few cottages. A hamlet more than a village.

'This is Staverton, such as it is.'

The brick wall turned a corner and then just stopped. There were two large brick gateposts, surmounted by lions, through which the jeep shot neatly forward into a long drive. Now they slowed, unable to avoid deep potholes.

If she had been told in the immediate aftermath of her conversation with Charles Masters the previous day to describe Staverton, she would probably have come up with a picture that resembled the larger villas on the western side of the lake in the suburbs of Chicago – spacious suburban grandeur. She would have envisaged trees, a large garden of perhaps two or three acres, possibly a pool, and/ or tennis courts. She would have described, in short, the sort of house after which her parents, before the ending of their marriage, had aspired in their wildest dreams, the house of a rich, successful bourgeois in the Western world. She would never, in spite of being warned in advance, have predicted this rutted drive that seemed, with each perilous swoop and dip of the jeep, to go on for ever. When they came in sight of the house, they turned rapidly into a gravelled forecourt so they still did not take in its size. This realisation was to come later.

At first glance, it did not appear as a house, still less as a home. The large red building climbing to Dutch gables above a second storey was more her idea of an institution, a sanatorium or a school, than a domestic residence. Sallie's eye took in an open door in a high brick wall. Through the door she could see outhouses, stables, paved yards. To the right, tall trees, a Spanish and a horse-chestnut on a big lawn, which stretched round the side of the house.

On a trampoline on the grass a child was bouncing up and down. Beside the trampoline stood a woman in a white roll-neck, jeans. To Sallie's amazement, this person was smoking a cigarette.

'Hi, Frannie!' Gloria called out. 'Hi, Jill.'

Jill was about Gloria's age, but less well preserved and her face was lined.

'Haven't you had a go, then?' Gloria quipped with her friend.

'Just been somersaulting, haven't I, Fran?'

Jill advanced, as Sallie walked towards them, and extended a hand. 'How do you do, welcome, I'm Jill.'

'Jill helps out two mornings a week,' said Gloria.

After the handshakes and the smiles, Jill was gone, a little too quickly, and Sallie was left to face her charge.

Now, she thought, *I could go, just now. I could ask for them to call a cab, say there'd been a mistake. Say anything.*

The child bounced one more time, on her bottom, then landed on her stockinged feet, before descending from the trampoline. She was a strikingly pretty redhead with very slightly curly, protuberant front teeth. In an older person such a mouthful would have made the face goofy, but in an eight-year-old the mouth was pretty. She smiled at the newcomer with her bright blue eyes. 'Is that all your luggage – in that backpack?'

'You should feel this!' Gloria told her, putting down the additional book bag.

'And I've a computer in here,' said Sallie, laying down the black plastic container.

'Cool,' said the little girl. 'I'm Frances, by the way.'

'Everyone calls her Fran or Frannie.'

'You do, Gloria.'

'What would you like me to call you? I'm Sallie, by the way.'

'I'd like you' – she giggled. 'It doesn't matter, but maybe Frances.'

'Maybe, Fran, you'd show Sallie her room? Help her settle in?'

'Okay!'

There was what seemed to be genuine friendliness in the child; certainly pleasure in a new face. 'Did Gloria tell you,' she asked, as she led the way towards the house. 'I helped make your bed? And we gathered flowers for your room. You don't have hay fever, do you?'

'No – why?'

'Only, Gloria said Americans are allergic to everything.'

'Hey!' called Gloria, who stared out this potentially embarrassing revelation without embarrassment. 'What happened to your shoes, young lady?'

Frances, clad in pink corduroy jeans, a flowery shirt, a dark-blue hand-knitted cardigan and polka-dot ankle socks, walked shoeless to the front door. It was a big, oak-panelled door with iron studs in it, looking as if it should have been opened to them by Boris Karloff. It was stone-mullioned and over it was a coat of arms and a motto in – Welsh? Certainly not Latin or Norman French.

'This part of the house is really old,' said the child, pushing the door. 'It was a bit of an older house, which got pulled down, so they added it to this house, when it was new. This is a nouve house, Daddy says.'

They were in a dark, panelled oak hall. Portraits, many obscured by brown Victorian varnish, peered from gold frames. The large hall contained some large sofas, low tables covered with magazines such as *Apollo*, *Connoisseur* and *Country Life*. At the bottom of the large staircase, which was also of oak, the panelling stopped abruptly.

'We could either go up this staircase, or up the back. Let's go this way, then you'll see more.'

'My God, how am I ever going to find my way around this place?'

'It depends how long you stay,' was the candid answer.

On the large landing at the top of this flight, Frances pointed to a door and said, 'That's my daddy's room. It was my mummy's *and* my daddy's but now it's just Daddy's.'

There was no obvious reply to this observation. They hurried on, insofar as the heavy luggage allowed speed, across the broad landing, down a few steps into a half-landing, up a narrower second flight of stairs – a servants' staircase? This led to another landing, which differed greatly from the oppressive grown-up quarters. Here were wall-to-wall carpeting, lighter paints. They passed, on one landing, a white bookcase filled with children's books. Sallie's eye caught Dr Seuss and Laura Ingalls Wilder.

'This is going to be your room,' said the child. 'You're quite near us, you see.'

Frances had led her into a room several times larger than the cramped Hackney place where Sallie had spent the previous three months. It was fitted out as a sitting room, with a writing table, a sofa, armchairs beside a fireplace, a television. With something of the hostess, and something of the estate agent, offering the property for sale, Frances said, 'and you've got a bedroom in here – and there's a bathroom off that.'

How many times had she made this speech? To how many nannies had she offered these courtesies?

'Oh, but hey, look at this view!'

From the window, Sallie saw a huge lawn, with high yews forming an avenue between their great squared cliffs. From another window could be seen a terrace and beyond that a deeply wooded valley stretching, seemingly limitlessly. No buildings, no railways, no roads, were visible, just a shimmering haze of trees, pale green with blossom and leaf, and the spring sky, and the powerful consoling strength, in bird and leaf and sky and branch, of Nature itself.

Chapter Five

'Now, you'll be all right on your own,' said Gloria.

Sallie was reminded of the way her mother used to speak to her at the school gate; Mother had meant to be kind, but a certain harshness would come into her tone when she said goodbye, desperate that Sallie would not make any kind of scene, or cling or weep.

'Don't forget – if there are any problems, if you are worried about *anything*, you've got our telephone number and you've got my cell number – and if you lose it . . .'

Frances chanted, 'It's written on the Remind Me list in the kitchen next to the fridge. Don't fuss, Gloria.'

'And I'll be round in the morning,' said Gloria, still addressing herself to Sallie. 'No need for you to worry about making breakfast. In fact, until we've worked out the alarm system a little better, it is really better you both stay upstairs until I come.'

Although these words had been uttered during, and after, the serving and consumption of high tea (tinned alphabet spaghetti) at the kitchen table, it was still hard to believe that they were true; that the two of them, Sallie and the child, were about to be left alone, in the unguarded, but electrically alarmed house, with its limitless corridors, landings and passageways. Only, in fact, when they stood by the door and watched the Japanese jeep scrunch the gravel, and turn out of sight down the drive, did the full reality of the situation dawn on Sallie.

She had thought that nervousness would subside when the other grown-up departed, and when she did not feel herself being constantly observed and assessed. But in fact, alone with Frances, she felt more nervous than ever. Charles Masters had placed a truly awesome burden upon her.

When the noise of the jeep faded to nothing, and all that was heard was the cawing of rooks in the chestnut trees upon the lawn and the distant whirr of an aeroplane in the clouds, the little girl looked at her winsomely and bit her lip.

All the time that Gloria was there, Frances had failed to engage with Sallie. The child had been perfectly polite and she had spoken when Sallie addressed remarks to her. But nothing like a rapport had yet been established. Now, this little smile had something in it of the coquette. It was not (of course it wasn't) a come-to-bed smile but children – it was one of the many things about them that Sallie found disconcerting and downright unamiable – have this way of flirting, of switching on a kind of ur-sexual charm. It was a little simper which said, 'Here we are. All alone. And what would you like to do?'

There were so many questions, Sallie realised, that she would like to have answered by Frances, but it would not do to blurt them out too soon. How had her mother died? What was it that had happened in Notting Hill when she and her brother had tried to spend a vacation in London? How rapid had been the turnover of previous nannies? And if there had been, as Sallie suspected, many young women coming and going, why did they not stay?

'We could play draughts, or chess, or Monopoly, or L'Attaque,' said Frances.

'What's L'Attaque?'

'It's like chess, only there are cardboard soldiers. And you don't know where the spies are, or where the mines are, so if you're a brigadier, say – that's really, really valuable – you can get blown sky-high. A sapper, and only a sapper, beats a mine.'

'Sounds complicated.'

'We could play something else.'

'No. I like complicated.' Sallie laughed.

It was decided, early as it was, to shut up, lock up and activate the alarm in the lower quarters of the house. The child showed an almost worrying competence in switching and turning the electronic devices.

'It's easy when you get to know it. If you are staying for long' – she simpered with a smile that was by no means unkind – 'then it's worth your learning how the alarm works, but if you're only going to be a week, let's say . . . Anyway, I'll do the alarm tonight,' said Frances with a slightly patronising smile. 'I'll explain it all properly in the morning. The thing is, you mustn't go downstairs, once the movement detectors are operating. You might not hear the alarm, but it will be activated. It rings in . . .' She whooped with laughter. 'We had one nannie, well, she was a temp, we *told* her about the alarm, but she probably didn't listen. I *think* she understood, but she was Hungarian. Daddy got her for a week. She went downstairs for something after we'd gone to bed. The police came from *Lymingbourne!*'

'I'll try not to make that mistake.'

Once in Frances's room, which was more like a little apartment, with its own electric kettle, its own fridge and supply of fruit and cookies, they played L'Attaque. The child was right, it was a good game, and Sallie thought it was a tribute to Frances that she could not tell whether the child allowed her new nanny to win the game out of politeness, or were they indeed quite evenly matched?

'Michael's really good at L'Attaque,' said Frances, 'but he is two years older.'

'I'm sure you're as good.'

'No,' said his sister without obvious rancour. 'He's better. He plays hard; he really, really plays to win.'

The little silence, before they said goodnight to one another, suggested that the two females should enjoy themselves before the return, or intrusion, of a male rival.

Chapter Six

In her own room, Sallie unzipped and disgorged the contents of the backpack. The splay of paperbacks and the printout of a draft thesis chapter, in its blue plastic cover case, were out of place here where books aplenty were shelved, or placed in little piles on tables around the room, for the sake of diversion or instruction, but not as vehicles for getting on. The books that furnished this room were not asking anyone to pit their wits against them.

Her draft chapter was provisionally called 'Metanym and Anonym'. Professor Helstone had ringed both words with pencil and written beside them, very neatly, 'Neither word is in my dictionary!' She had tried to set out, in this chapter, the idea that the namelessness of the governess, and the namelessness of her employer, in *The Turn of the Screw* were essential ingredients in the tale's power.

Baudrillard had argued (*Simulations*, 1983) that in hyper-real situations, what is real and what is imaginary implode into one another. We experience 'reality' and 'simulations' as 'hyperreality', without being able to distinguish between them. To judge from some of the neatly pencilled question marks in her margin, as from the ambiguous grunts which

Professor Helstone emitted when she had tried to expound these ideas orally, she had wondered whether her supervisor had actually read, or even heard of, Baudrillard's *Simulations*. He had told her, prosaically, that in an opening chapter it was necessary to be much, much clearer about her methodology. She must set out, intelligibly, what it was that she was intending to say in all the subsequent hundred thousand words, and give some indication of how she was going to present her case.

Sallie had tried to explain. Her point was, you could not tell, from the way that Henry James had written his story, whether the governess, the narrator of all the horrible events, was recounting something that had actually happened, or something she just dreamt up out of her head. That is obvious and must have occurred to any reader of *Turn*, however unsophisticated.

The story is read aloud to a group of *men* at a house party. It is the written testimony of the governess, who is now dead, of what had occurred when she was engaged by her employer to go down to Bly, in Essex, to look after two children, Miles and Flora.

The salient facts about the governess's story are explained by the narrator. That is, she had never told anyone orally about the uncanny experiences since they happened. (She told the old housekeeper while they were happening, but we do not have Mrs Grose the housekeeper's independent or corroborative evidence for this.) Then there is the fact that Douglas, the member of the house party who reads the story aloud, had clearly been a little in love with the governess; she was his sister's governess. But he had never spoken about the supernatural experiences with her. He was 'at Trinity' while the governess looked after his kid sister and he had not discussed the matter with anyone in the last forty years. That means he is now round about sixty when he is reading the governess's story to the fellow guests at the house party one Christmas time. And her story is written 'in old faded ink, and in the most beautiful hand'.

But when he has finished reading the story, we never return to the circle of friends round the fireside; we never hear their reaction, nor whether any of them find it plausible. All we are left with at the end is the governess, distraught, holding in her arms the body of a dead child – a dead little boy.

James's story, Sallie argued in her draft chapter, was a classic example of Baudrillard's 'hyperreality'. Helstone wanted her to mention the fact that James himself, in the notebooks, remarks that he wants to heighten the terror and the reality, how he wants to make it clear that the ghosts are real. Helstone seemed to think these bits of bio-graphical trivia were going to substantiate the case she was making rather than being, as she supposed, quite irrelevant to it. Sallie was not trying to sit down and write some kind of middle-brow biographical criticism. She was attempting a reading of *Turn* as a text about the irrelevance of applying truth criteria to narratives, whether metanarratives such as Darwinian science or Marxist political theory, or smaller ones, like a woman saying she'd seen ghosts. She was no more interested in the *author* of *Turn* than she was in the 'fictitious' group assembled at the commencement of the text to hear 'Douglas's narrative'.

Helstone had changed 'commencement' to 'beginning' and every time she had spoken of *Turn*, he had added the words 'of the Screw' in his neat pencilled hand. This in itself was a source of dismay to her, since he seemed not to realise that there was something very deliberate in her truncating, and hence renaming, the text. Apart from his pedantic pencillings, he had ridiculously little to contribute to her scheme and she felt very badly let down by him. To have crossed the Atlantic, and endured months of loneliness and cold and near nervous collapse for this! He had tried to persuade her to read a philosophical text called *Appearance and Reality*, which he said was relevant to her theme. He said that it was in order to be taught by the author of this text that T. S. Eliot had – and he'd smirked as at some private joke, Helstone – made the same journey as herself and come to England. The author, he'd said, was called Bradley, but he did not wish to paraphrase his viewpoint until she had tasted the book for herself. It had been written contemporaneously with James (this historicist mania!). And it would, he hoped she would agree, turn out to be helpful to her.

Sallie, if the truth were told, knew that she had not yet discovered her theme. She was still thrashing about. She was very resistant, however, to forcing her mind into Hell's Tone's groove. She felt that if she were to do so, and to begin reading *Turn* by his relentlessly historicist and realist frames of reference, in short if she were to attempt to 'make sense' of the text, she would somehow be missing its point. She would be not merely missing the point of Henry James, but of the whole reading experience. The previous five years of beginning to learn the strange new language of 'theory' would be lost to her. It was the resistance to 'sense', or 'making sense', which had inspired her to choose the unintelligible title 'Metanym and Anonym'. *Turn* was itself a turn, in which metaphor and the nominal, the real and the imagined, imploded classically: hence 'metanym', a change or turn of name. 'Anonym'? The governess's namelessness is both a fact – that was surely realist enough for Hell's

Bells? But it was also in itself a metaphor. Everything was a metaphor – what else was language? You could tear up the dictionary now. Too much tying up of ends, too much attempt to find words in the ancient classifications of etymological 'definition' would destroy precisely what she was setting out to do. Language was free. Walk about the city and most of the words coming into your head, jingle-jangle, randomly, were incomprehensible. We were back in Babel. The growth of dictionaries was something which was a phenomenon of the Enlightenment, a male attempt, like the invention of encyclopaedias, to classify and arrange reality in alphabetical order. But James's young woman, coming into a household of ghosts and children, has upset all that old hierarchy of language and meaning, and discovers something completely new. She's not walking about a city clutching an *A to Z*. Who said A came 'before' Z? God?

Hell's Stones had mumbled something about it being one thing for the *governess* not to be able to distinguish between Appearance and Reality, but it was quite another thing for *us* to be in the same predicament. With one of his nasal harrumphs, he had said that in his own reading experience he had found dictionaries, with their definitions, rather – and what was it about this word which provoked in him such self-satisfied smirks and such private laughter? – *useful*!

Yet now, in a quite different way, she was inside *Turn*! In life, she had become the governess and Staverton did, really, bear some astonishing resemblances to Bly, the old house in James's story. It is true that she had been hired, not by a remote guardian of the children but by their own father. And compared with the governess's shadowy obsession with the man who hired her, Sallie's relationship with

Charles Masters was already well advanced – in some ways he had forced the pace too alarmingly. Yet, where Hell's Teeth had failed to persuade her to be interested historically or realistically in Henry James, his world, his circle and the actual circumstances of the story, Charles Masters had succeeded. Now, in the lamplight of her bedroom-study at Bly, the arid weeks of staring at a laptop in the British Library became very remote. And so did the thesis. Its very language seemed odd to her, as she turned the pages of the draft chapter, and she began to ask herself whether she had not (together with all her friends in the Group) been trying to use such language as a way of disguising from herself the absence of any substantial or original thoughts.

Seeing her garish American paperbacks, and the chapter, spread out upon the bed at Bly made her think of them as messages from another age or planet, scarcely decipherable in the context of this room, with its old-fashioned furniture, its comfortable and faded chintz. Its very books drew her into a new realm. The novels were chiefly in the English comic tradition. There was Waugh here and P. G. Wodehouse, a novelist she had never tried before. The more substantial volumes were political biographies. She did not know much about Churchill or Roosevelt, though these were names which, at least, she recognised. Some of the other biographical subjects, such as Garibaldi, or Massingberd, were a little harder to place. Garibaldi? An opera star?

She gathered up her own paperbacks and arranged them in a row on the writing table against the wall, with its sand-coloured wallpaper and its grey trellis pattern. She laid the thesis chapter on the blotter. Maybe she'd get some ideas about how to continue it if she stayed here at Bly not just a few weeks, but a few months, began to acclimatise, to assimilate, to learn the language of England and its country-side, which outside, in the dark of thick trees and wet sky, still retained its mystery, just as the English child, surely now asleep in its room, retained its?

She had drunk coffee with Frances while they played L'Attaque and the caffeine had put Sallie into a hyperactive mental condition. Her heart was pounding. Her mind raced. She was alone, in this enormous place, with the child, and the excitement pounded in her head and chest. There was no possibility of calming down sufficiently to read, let alone to sleep. She feared to switch on the tele-vision. Although Flora had said that she 'slept through anything', Sallie thought that the throbbing sound of a television in a nearby room would disturb the child. More than this, she dreaded watching television on her own. It was something quite frightening, to be exposed to all that the television could throw at you – just sitting there, vulner-able to its images and noises and fantasies.

The house was what was calling her. Without the child, and without Gloria's searching gaze, she wanted to explore.

Little Flora had made it clear that the staircase and the lower regions of Bly were alarmed, but that still left the upper storeys. There was a flashlight beside her bed and she took this on to the landing, where everything was now dark. The child must have switched the light out. Sallie herself did not recollect doing so. The child's bedroom door was two along from her own and, as she paused beside it, Sallie intuited, from the silence, that the little girl was already 'sleeping through anything'. The red head would be limp on the pillow, its throat so vulnerable, its gurgling breath so like a baby's.

Sallie knew most specifically what it was that she wanted,

what she had to do. She had wanted to do it, indeed, for the last few hours, ever since the child had told her *That's my daddy's room. It was my mummy's and my daddy's, but now it's just Daddy's.*

The flashlight guided Sallie down the first, the narrow staircase, at the bottom of which she took a right. Her prime concern was that she should not stray into any area that was covered by the burglar alarm system, but she was fairly certain that so long as she avoided the main staircase and did not go down it, she would not set any bells ringing.

With the specific fear of setting off the alarm, there was mingled a generalised fear occasioned by the darkness and by the strangeness of it all. Now that she was on the bigger landing, she found herself approaching a large low-lying window, which admitted the eerie light of the moon through light rain. Extinguishing the flashlight, she looked out on the garden, at the high hedges, the topiary and the wet lawns, which gleamed and glistened silvery white. Though she could see that everything outside was wet, the cold light appeared to turn everything to ice. She looked as if on a frozen world. And she shuddered, with cold and with fear.

When she once again switched on the flashlight, there was a moment when it blinded, destroying the light of the moon and only emphasising, beyond its own yellow focus, a universal blackness indoors. In that darkness she could hear creaking, somewhere down the end of the corridor, and she sensed that someone was there.

What had the child added, when she had told Sallie about her father's room? 'Now it's just Daddy's – when he's here.'

'When he's here . . . Daddy's room . . . when he's here . . .'

Sallie stood still in the darkness and waited for a repetition of the creaking floorboard, or door hinge, or whatever the noise had been at the end of the passage. But there was just silence. It was still possible that there was someone there and she tried to listen for the sound of another person breathing. Perhaps, though, this Other was holding his breath and listening for her? Waiting for her? An armed intruder? A thief? Or was there someone else in this house she hadn't been told about? Or had the child woken up and come down the landing following her, spying on her, seeing what she was up to? Maybe all the nannies were intent on doing what she was just about to do?

Afterwards, when she framed the memory of that first evening at Staverton, she was able to offer herself explanations of why she had been so frightened, and they were of the kind just itemised. While she was actually standing there in the darkness, though, the thoughts – that the presence was a Someone, a child, a burglar, Charles himself, watching her – had not formed articulately in her head; they had come all in a jangle, unarranged as darts shot out of a jungle at a lost explorer.

The flashlight danced from door to door.

Daddy's room.

When he's here. It was Mummy's . . . Now it's just Daddy's, when he's here.

Or this? Or this?

With all the lights switched on, it would have been easy to distinguish, but in the dark, on an unfamiliar landing, it was much less easy. She tried one doorknob. Turning it at that midnight hour and in that silence, it seemed as if the crack it made was as loud as gunfire. The floorboards creaked so loudly they could have been booby-trapped.

The flashlight made a quick trip round the room just

penetrated and made out high twin beds separated by a bedside table. It was a very large room, with a fireplace at one end, armchairs, but this . . . couldn't have been . . . his. A spare room. Closing the door as carefully as she could, the handle and latch were once more gunshot loud.

The child had made her little remark beside her father's bedroom door and this had been just before they had turned to ascend the second, the servants' staircase. So the door that contained him – 'when he's here' – must be near. Sallie tried another handle. Locked. She came back into the corridor, turned and realised that in the dark she had lost her bearings. She had, in fact, come all the way back to her own, that is to the little narrow staircase. It was while facing that staircase that Flora had made her remarks. So – yes, she remembered now, if she turned and went back about ten yards down this strip of carpet . . . She was here.

The door of the master bedroom was large, imposing. The handle, when she held it, appeared to be huge, a ribbed metallic knob. Like the other door she had opened by mistake, this too opened noisily but with nothing like the same gunfire clatter. The hinges were smooth, the door swung. She immediately smelt that she was in the right place.

The room was not unpleasantly smelly. There was nevertheless a quite unmistakable masculine aroma. No woman's room ever smelt like this. To a combination of leather and the very faint mustiness of worsted suspended from coat-hangers in closets there was blended some distinctively masculine soap or cologne. She closed the door behind her and inhaled gaspingly, not to savour the smell of the place but to prevent herself from passing out with overexcitement.

She longed to see the room. But if she switched on the

light, would she be seen from the garden or the park beyond? And be taken for an intruder? Yet, most passionately, she needed to see the room, to investigate it, *to read it.*

Then, to her horrified amazement, she found herself staring at another woman, who stood there and flashed an electric torch at her. It was impossible not to gulp, gasp at the sight. She could not make the woman out, though she could see that it was a woman. The flashlight, which caught Sallie's eyes and sometimes blinded her, quivered and shook.

A mirror. One of those long dressing mirrors on a swivel. When she had recovered from this very nasty surprise, Sallie became desperate to switch on a sidelight. She needed light as a lost traveller in a desert might need water. Hyperventilated, she also needed water. Trying to avoid the mirror which, although she now recognised it for what it was, had not lost its power to be alarming, she played the flashlight round the room in search of what she needed. Eventually she found a table, a large pile of books and a lamp. Treading as gingerly as a spy, flashlighting now the space in front of her, now her feet, she shuffled carefully, dreading a collision with a heavy object of furniture.

She fiddled with a switch but nothing happened. Her hands had found a lamp, or that was what it felt like. The switch was unfamiliar and, as she held the large metallic circle between her fingers, she could not figure whether you squeezed it, yanked it or twisted it. Sure as hell the one thing you weren't meant to do was break it.

'Shit,' she whispered.

There was nothing for it but to do another shuffle back towards the door in the dark and find a wall switch. This journey back took what felt like for ever. She hardly dared to move more than an inch at a time and at some points she wondered whether she was in fact going back towards the door, or had somehow managed to get herself facing the wrong way. But, having stubbed her toe once or twice against sharp edges of furniture, and ruckled carpets with feet too timid to lift, she eventually found herself nosed against a wall, and tremulous fingers discovered what they so desperately wanted.

It was a considerably larger room than her own. A four-poster bed, hung with old red damask, stood in the centre. At its end was the table, with blotter and inks and envelopes, and the Victorian reading lamp which she had tried previously and without success to turn on. There was a large mahogany door in the corner of the room, and opening that she found a further room, with a small bed made up and a huge wardrobe taking up the whole of one wall. As in the other room, there was a full-length mirror, this time in the door of the wardrobe. She smiled back nervously at herself a flirty smile, conspiratorial, which said, 'Hey, Sal, what are you doin'?' In her T-shirt, jeans and white socks she looked sheepishly young. For a moment, her shy smile broadened to a grin. If They could see her now! – Mom, Lorrie, the Group!

Beyond the dressing room a further door led into the bathroom. She spent some time there, staring soulfully into the glass over the basin and stroking her cheeks with his thick badgery shaving brush. She unscrewed the cap of his cologne bottle and dabbed some on an ear lobe. She slowly and gently put his toothbrush in her mouth, first cleaning her teeth with and then gently sucking the bristle. She tried to assess the likelihood, if she stole it, of its being missed. Surely he would just get another from the closet? Then she considered the possibility of his anger upon finding it missing and decided to leave it, but not before savouring it on gum and tongue, and trying, through the taste of toothpaste, to make out the much more beguiling taste of him.

So far, so good. Her fear had painted a bathroom with evidence of a female presence. There were no girly things here, no lipsticks, no tampons. If women ever came here, they were his visitors, not residents. What about *her* – the wife? Had she used this bathroom, or was it so grand a house that they had His'n'Hers?

It was only when Sallie came back into the bedroom that she saw Her, and wondered how she could have missed Her when the lights first went on. For there she was, quite dominating the room from her silver frame on the dressing table opposite the bed. You could see there was a look of Flora in that face, with its hair in a headband and curling lips. The brow of the nose was the same too, identical. God damn it, he must love Flora for looking so like her mother! Or did the sight of the girl cause him pain – was that why he could not come down here any more? Which?

The woman in the photograph was smiling. It was not a grin, you could not see teeth, but she smiled with her eyes as well as her lips. Sallie felt herself being watched by those smiling eyes. She stared back. She faced the dead woman out. Her initial shock at being stared at by Charles Masters's dead wife was overtaken by poignant sensations.

Had the woman in the photograph been elevated into the iconic status of the saint? If so, no one could compete with her and she, Sallie, would never be to Charles what this poised and damned-perfect English lady still was, and always would be. These thoughts were so crushing that for a moment or two of shock, as she stared transfixed at the silver frame, Sallie wanted to run, to abandon the competition, to recognise that she would never *have* Charles. But her sense of inadequacy was interfused with one of robustness: not for nothing had Sallie Declan been born in Defiance.

'I have one thing you don't have,' she whispered. 'I am alive.'

What remembrances of her, what physical mementoes, had he retained? Clothes? Nighties of hers which, lying in this large bed, he hugged to himself tearfully?

Sallie strode back towards the dressing room and threw open the wardrobe door, no longer minding how much noise she might be making. Had there been women's dresses here, it might have been difficult to stomach. There were, rather, about ten men's suits neatly hanging, a variety of tweedy coats, all beautifully cleaned and brushed. On the wardrobe floor were four highly polished pairs of black shoes, stiffened by their shoehorns, and two pairs of brown, glistening like new-burst chestnuts. Behind another door of the closet were socks, shorts, sweaters. *Gloria, damn.*

Gloria had been in here. No man kept his things so neat. Gloria's hands had touched this underwear, these shirts, this nightwear.

Sallie's hands stroked, then lifted, then took, a striped pyjama top. What the hell?

Back in the bedroom, she stood in front of the long swivel mirror and surveyed, half with sensual pleasure and half with the curiosity of a stranger, the narrow bony shoulders and almost non-existent breasts which were exposed by the removal of the T-shirt. She put on the top. Then she removed jeans, socks, panties, and stood for some time in the range of the looking-glass. The white thighs that came down beneath the pyjama jacket were interrupted in the middle by a tiny hamster of fluff. Her legs were okay. Turning to inspect the butt, she raged again at that poisonous Kenner kid. A kid who said words like that deserved to be hit. A mother who raised a kid who could say such things deserved to be frightened a little. Sallie's mother had heard – some kind citizen of Muncie had reported it back to her – that the blood came through the paintwork of Mrs Kenner's bathroom even when she'd had it redecorated. That, she told herself, as she looked at it, is a full, beautiful bottom. It is not a fat butt. The face which had popped out of the pyjama top and was staring back at her with a childish overexcitement was a new Sallie, a Sallie reborn with fresh confidence. Go on, its expression seemed to say, just watch me. Watch me, dead lady! Watch me get into your husband's bed. My bed now. Go ahead.

She drew back the red damask covers. Beneath, clean sheets and immaculate blankets. She climbed in between them. A wall switch by the bed turned off all the lights in the room. For a while, darkness was total, but the eyes got used to it and the faint moonlight from the windows made the shape of the room quite clear to her from the pillows where she lay. Now that she knew what the room looked like, she could envisage, from her vantage point, the tables and chairs, which before had been dark lumps in a greater dark. The fine linen sheets were very cold against her bare legs; cold, but deliciously so.

Chapter Seven

'So, is it a story you're writing on your computer?'

'More like, a story about a story.'

'I don't understand.'

'It's kind of like . . . well, long, long ago, there was this really amazing storyteller.'

'Have you read the Harry Potter books?'

Sallie had not, so Frances told her the story of the first one. Explaining the nature of the academy, and of the magic, took them from the sundial on the terrace, which they closely inspected, to a fishpond and beyond that to a shrubbery where rhododendrons were beginning to come into flower. The size and extent of the garden were truly astounding. Charles, during their interview, had warned her that Staverton was a place where they 'rattled around a bit', and he had spoken of the garden as being 'more than they could handle'. Her mind had nevertheless persisted, all the way down in the train, in painting images of suburban prosperity: a tennis court or a pool, perhaps, but nothing on this scale, this huge acreage of lawns and tended beds, these miles of woodland and field beyond.

While the child chattered on about her favourite books, Sallie meditated upon the problem of how you would explain *Turn* to an eight-year-old. For so long, now, she had been rereading the text, teasing out its ambiguities, mastering the daunting extent of secondary literature, that part of her difficulty would consist in compressing what she had to say into comprehensible terms. The other problem was more acute. How could you, without the risk of causing real alarm, convey just how goddamned scary the story was? It wasn't just scary because it was a story about ghosts. It was scary because of the suppressed violence that shimmered beneath its elegant sentences. Once you had read it, you could never forget its climax, a little boy falling back dead in the arms of the woman who had been hired to look after him. And we only ever have her word for it that he died of fright, or strain imposed by the ghosts . . .

Frances turned to her and said, 'So maybe you'll read it? I can lend it to you if you like. Then we can talk about it. And you'd have something to talk about to Michael – otherwise he'll just try to talk about football and cricket when he comes back from school.'

'I'd love that.'

'She's written *Harry Potter and the Philosopher's Stone, Harry Potter and the Goblet of Fire* . . .'

'Maybe I'll start with the first in the series.'

'Then there's *Harry Potter and the Chamber of Secrets* and *Harry Potter and the Prisoner of Azkaban, Harry Potter and the Order of the Phoenix.*'

'Which is the best?'

Frances smiled enigmatically. At first Sallie expected the child to confess that the choice was a difficult one, but then she made it clear that such an approach to her favourite author was not one she chose to make. 'They're all cool, but you're right. You have to start at the beginning. You still haven't told me what your story is called.'

'My thesis – my book? Or the one I'm writing about?'

'Either.'

'Well, mine's called Meta –' her courage failed. If Helstone couldn't swallow the title what would the kid make of it? 'The story I'm writing about was called *The Turn of the Screw*.'

'Who wrote it?'

'Henry James.'

'Is it a ghost story?'

This was a disconcertingly accurate first shot.

'Well, yes it is.'

'Did he write it a really, really, long time ago?'

'A bit over a hundred years ago.'

'I expect it's in the house, Daddy has most of the stories of long ago. It's just the new ones like Harry Potter we have to send out for. So is it scary, *The Turn of the Screw*?'

'Yes, really, really scary'.

Frances began to shudder melodramatically, like a kid doing trick or treat on Hallowe'en. 'Is it,' she persisted, 'a haunted house?'

'A haunted house – a haunted garden – the whole place is haunted.'

Frances had had her turn. She made it clear that it was now for Sallie to tell a story, as they turned through the shrubbery down muddy, root-broken paths, in a broad circuit that encompassed the front of the house and led them down a long gravelled walk, bordered on one side by a high brick wall.

'There used to be greenhouses here in the olden days, but Daddy had to pull them all down, they were so broken.

They were really good ones. They grew peaches and other fruit. And all this was a big kitchen garden.'

Most of the kitchen garden, though kept neat enough, was now uncultivated, but there were some rows of onions and some potatoes.

'Anyway,' persisted Frances, 'tell me your ghost story.'

'Well, there's this young woman.'

'Called?'

'She doesn't have a name – or anyway, we aren't told it.'

'Isn't that quite strange? We all have names.'

'Henry James doesn't tell us.'

'Shouldn't he have? J. K. Rowling gives names to all the characters.'

Sallie suppressed annoyance. She could see that Henry James was about to be pitted against J. K. Rowling in a competition by whose narrow set of rules he was bound to lose.

'Anyhow, whatever her name was, there's this young woman and she goes down to a big house in the country to look after two children, a little girl and a little boy.'

'Is that why you wanted to come here, to look after us – so you could be like the lady in your story?'

This enquiry flustered Sallie. She did not know the answer and during her spluttered 'No, no – no, not at all,' the little girl smiled knowingly. 'Why is it a ghost story?' she persisted.

'Well, not long after she's arrived in the house, the young woman, the governess . . .'

'Who happens to have no name! Fishy!'

'. . . who has a name but we aren't told it . . .'

'Because Henry James forgot to tell us.'

'. . . she arrives in the house and she starts . . . she starts seeing . . . First she sees a man on this tower at the end of the house. And then she sees him again, staring at her through the dining-room window . . .'

'And is he really a ghost?'

'Yes – he's a ghost.'

'Scary . . . ooooh!'

It was hard to know this time whether beneath the melodramatic expressions of terror there was not also true fear.

The little girl danced with a slightly mad frenzy, tugging at her long straight red hair. 'I'm the ghost of the man! The ma-a-a-a-an! And I suppose he had no name either, because lazybones Henry James couldn't be bothered to think up a name for him?'

'Oh that's just *it*! He thinks up names, wonderful, witty names which are appropriate for nearly all his characters. And the ghosts – because there are two ghosts. The lady ghost is the person who used to look after the two children before – she's called Miss Jessel. And the man ghost is called Peter Quint.'

'Why is that witty?'

'Because Quint sounds like he's squinty, looking at you; because it sounds like a number of other . . . well, bad things.'

'What bad things?'

'I can't say.'

'And what happens in the end?'

'That I can't say either.'

'Haven't you read to the end yet?'

'I have read it many times. I remember all too clearly what happens in the end.'

'Is it too scary to tell?'

'Yes. Yes, it is. And it's, it's also . . .'

'What?'

'Too *terrible*.'

Later that day they disobeyed Gloria's house rules and separated. Sallie was conscious that the child did not want her around all the time and when Frances said she thought she'd go to her room, it seemed a good moment for an hour or two apart. She remembered that Daddy had most of the stories of long ago and thought she would explore the library, which led off the drawing room.

It was a large, forbiddingly brown room lined with books. Sure enough, on one shelf she found complete sets of Conrad, Galsworthy, George Meredith and a large blue set, with spines pricked out in gilt: the works of the Master. The library steps were on casters and she trundled them to the appropriate section of the dusty shelves. Beneath the sets of Edwardian fiction were works of mid-twentieth-century popular history, Churchill's *History of the English Speaking Peoples*, Rowse on the Elizabethans, Cecil Woodham Smith's *The Reason Why* and Arthur Bryant's volumes on Pepys.

She ascended, steadying herself by grasping the rounded pole that grew from the top step and, as she stretched towards a volume of Henry James, the telephone rang.

She had not noticed that there was a phone in the room, but looking down into the library's shadowy glooms, she made out what looked like a fax machine and probably an answerphone. It gave half a dozen rings, and she was beginning to ask herself whether she should climb down and answer it, when the machine clicked into life and she heard his voice.

'Gloria – it's Charles here. Something's cropped up and it isn't helped by the fact that I'm actually leaving for Hong Kong this evening. So if you could give me a ring back, I'd be most . . .'

'Hello, Charles.'

'Oh, Gloria, good.'

'Just chopping onions. Sorry not to have come to the phone sooner.'

'That's okay.'

'I'm making them a cottage pie. Hope that's all right. You never know what Americans will eat.'

'Gloria, this case.'

'Oh, yes.' There was a weary resignation, tinged with heavy irony, as she said this.

'There's been the most almighty cock-up with our office at the other end and the simple fact is, Gloria, I'm going to have to be out there for at least six weeks. Now, it's possible I shall get back before that for a weekend to see the kids and I feel dreadful about . . .'

'Hey ho.'

'Gloria?'

'Frankly, Charles, I had expected this.'

Following the silence, he said, 'Gloria?'

'I'm here. I'm listening.'

'Look. I feel terrible about this.'

'There's one obvious solution,' said Gloria's voice.

He came back very firmly. 'Gloria, we've discussed that and it isn't a road I'm going down. You know that.'

There was a very long silence.

'So,' he asked. The bitch wasn't making things easy for him. 'So how are things working out?'

'With the American girl?'

'Basically, yes.'

'Well, Mike's not back from school yet, is he? We'll have to see. That'll be make or break time. She's a nice enough person, I dare say. Very shy, a bit wrapped up in herself, not at all your brash American type. Frannie's being great.'

'She always is.'

'Trying to draw her out, make her feel at home. You'd think Fran was the grown-up and Sallie was the kid, really. Frannie thinks maybe we should get her to go riding with them when Mike gets back from school. Americans like riding, don't they – Wild West 'n' all?'

'It might be a very good thing. A good way of seeing the country, always, from the back of a horse.'

'We must make sure she can ride – after the last one?'

'Gloria, I wouldn't be asking you to do this if . . .'

'I do understand, Charles. But on the other hand you've got to understand, Ken and I aren't going to sacrifice our marriage for you, Charles. I'm sorry to put it as crudely as that but . . .'

There was a long silence.

'Of course you can't do that, Gloria. I'm not asking that. Look, as soon as this case is over, I promise you we'll put everything on a very different footing. We'll get a full-time, live-in au pair. This girl, Sallie, the American – you don't see her as settling down in that position?'

'Well . . .'

'Gloria, she's okay? There's nothing funny about her? There's nothing you should be telling me?'

'How d'you mean, Charles? Don't you mean there's something *you* should be telling *me*?'

'Of course not. Only, if anything did go wrong in the next few weeks . . .'

'Have you told her you want her for a few weeks?'

'I thought at first, you see, we'd only need her for a fortnight. I thought maybe you could have a word with her. If it doesn't work out, we have to go back to the agency . . .'

'Back to Edith – Margarita? – Nathalie? Mike saw them all off. No, Charles, we can't go down that road again and

I'm telling you, I can't stay in the house overnight any more, l can't . . .'

'I'm not asking that, Gloria. And by the way. I don't think Michael saw them off, exactly. I think we just had bad luck with those particular girls.'

'Three holidays running? They can go and play at Lucy's house, you don't mind that?'

'So long as they stay with Lucy's mum or their nanny, but they must be supervised at all times.'

'Of course.'

'That is essential. Look' – he cleared his throat – 'I'm sure everything's fine with this American girl, but there is something I've got to tell you about her.'

'Oh my Gawd!' Gloria cackled. 'No, no, don't tell me!'

'It's just her references. I've rung her professor in London. Between you and me he sounds like a basket case, yammering about the subject matter of her thesis being perhaps too appropriate. But it's the American reference that worries me. She gave me the number of a Mrs Margaret Kenner. When I rang it, I got a message which said "Lorrie can't take your call right now". Lorrie, not Margaret. When I finally got through, Mrs Kenner sounded . . . well, a bit confused. Said she was happy to vouch for Sallie but couldn't give me any examples of how she'd been good with kids. Said she had two children and in Sallie's interview she said she'd only looked after one. And then I checked the area code. Mrs Kenner is supposed to live in Muncie, Indiana and the number I'd been ringing turned out upon enquiry to be Carver, Ohio.'

'So you're saying Sallie faked her references?'

'It's probably perfectly all right. I expect there will turn out to be an adequate explanation, but just for the moment, Gloria, could you be especially . . .'

The tape clicked to the end. The conversation had used up the whole of the tape on the answering machine. How much longer Charles and Gloria continued their conversation Sallie would not know. She sat at the top of the library steps, clutching *The Turn of the Screw* and staring blankly across the room.

Chapter Eight

Hey, Lorrie. Listen. You're not answering my e-mails. This is important, Lorrie. I've decided to stay at Staverton. I know (don't ask how) that Charles Masters has been in touch with you. If he phones again, make some excuse. Say there's been a mistake. A wrong number. Anything. Listen, Lorrie. It was really stupid of me to ask you to impersonate Mrs Kenner and I should never have done it, okay? I really, really want this thing to work out, this assignment for Charles and his kids.

It seems so funny, we made all those jokes before I came to England about me being like some Henry James heroine coming to Europe from the US!! We tried on the Isabel Archer for a fit, no go. I don't think I'm exactly Charlotte in the GB, either!!! The one we didn't dream of was me walking right into the middle of *Turn*!!! Seriously, Staverton's not too like Bly, though I mix them up sometimes. Frances, that's the little girl I look after, asked me the other day, 'Why do you call me Flora sometimes?' Jesus, Lorrie, she really and truly asked that! So I must be careful. Miles, the elder brother, came back from his boarding school two days ago and I started calling him Miles straight away. My God, I've done it again. Michael, Michael, Michael, he's called Michael. He's a polite kid, and he smiled and said quietly, 'I don't really like teasing.' Poor little man, I bet they tease the hell out of him at his school. Anyway he asked me about *Turn* and I said, 'At least you haven't been thrown out of your school for bad things, like Miles in the story.' And this boy, Michael, asks me, 'Like, what bad things had Miles done?'

I explained that in the Henry James story the lady looking after the kids gets this letter from the school asking her not to send Miles back, but it isn't explained what bad things he's supposed to have done – not in the letter. Only at the very end does Miles start referring to the school himself. So I told Miles the story, like I'd told it to Frances, a watered-down version. I found myself telling it like it was just a real, old-fashioned ghost story. You know, Lorrie, on one level that is all it is. I realised this, trying to tell the kids about it. But all the time I was telling the boy the story, I was conscious that I was going to have to lie to him about the end. No way was I going to tell Michael that little Miles dies. And it never struck me so strongly before that this is just the governess's word against everyone else's. We just have her word for it that there were ghosts, and that the children were talking to the ghosts and somehow got sucked into their evil. But imagine what a jury would make of that if she had been on trial for homicide! We have her word for it that Miles's heart stops beating because of his terrifying vision of Mr Quint. Supposing there's some other reason for the child's death?

Anyway, this is a long way from Mrs Kenner and those references. I'm due to go riding in ten minutes. Christ, I hope the instructor doesn't let go of my horse's head. Please be in touch, Lorrie, this is important to me.

Chapter Nine

Michael Masters was a delicate-looking, thin child who looked younger than ten. He had the red hair and toothy mouth of his sister, but his face was longer, distinctly reminiscent in its bone structure of his father. A disconcerting feature of his face was that it sometimes wore an expression of apparent agony. The first few times Sallie had seen this she had wondered whether the boy was holding back tears, but he would sometimes be about to laugh. It was a strange look, caused by a combination of nervously pulling back the corners of his lips and slightly tautening his eye muscles. Obviously he did not know he was doing it and, because she had only known him two days, she still had not come to any conclusions about it. Was he, perhaps, a truly melancholic or difficult boy? It was not reassuring to know that in his father's opinion at least, Michael had 'seen off' three predecessors.

Michael, wearing a velvet riding cap, jeans which looked as if they might fall off his skinny hips, a red-and-white checked shirt and a dark-blue sweater, was standing in the cobbled stable yard. 'Oh, good,' he said, when Sallie appeared. 'We thought you might not be coming.'

During her brief period of taking riding lessons at
Muncie, the drill had been gentle. Someone brought a
little pony to you, all ready saddled and bridled. They
helped you climb on to it and, for the first few lessons, they
led you round and round in a circle. More advanced
equestrian students broke into a trot and began to learn
dressage. Sallie imagined, hoped, that some such arrangement
was going to be in evidence here.

'Sallie can take Peperoni,' she could hear Gloria's voice.

'We both have our own ponies,' said Michael helpfully.
'They are Welsh ponies. Rob looks after them for us when
we're at school. You've met Rob?'

'Hello!'

Sallie had not met Rob before, even though she had now
been at Staverton for four days and five nights.

He was a tall, balding man, with slightly crinkly dark hair
clinging to the sides of his head. He had not shaved for a
couple of days and he had what would, in a fashion photo,
be called designer stubble. He had an open-necked shirt,
which revealed a hairy chest, and he wore jeans and rubber
boots. He was aged about forty. The hand that grasped hers
was very strong and the nails were black with earth. He had
dark gypsy eyes. 'The horses are nearly ready for you.'

Frances was leading out her pony, a stocky little brown
animal whom she introduced as Potter.

'How many hands do you think he is?' Michael challenged her.

'Who, me?' Sallie giggled.

'You're the one I asked.'

Sallie didn't want to say that she had no idea what a
hand in this context measured. 'I couldn't say, I . . .'

'How many hands do you normally ride?' persisted
Michael.

'Peperoni's sixteen hands,' said Rob, looking at her carefully. 'You've ridden a hunter before?'

'We wouldn't have called it that,' said Sallie.

'Why not?' asked Michael. 'If that was what it was?'

'Maybe you call them something different in America,' said Rob.

She could not tell whether he was trying to rescue her, or ganging up with the little boy.

'Potter's about, what do you say, Rob, twelve-two?' said the boy.

'Yup,' said Rob. 'And what about Joystick?'

'He's thirteen,' said Michael.

'That's his age?'

'No, he's about ten. I'll show you.'

The boy ran into the stable and came out leading Joystick, another Welsh pony, but less tubby than his sister's.

Gloria emerged, holding various pieces of tackle, a saddle and some straps. 'Here you are, young man,' she said, half throwing them towards Michael.

With great proficiency Michael put the bridle over the horse's head and began buckling on his saddle. While he did so, his sister was at work getting Potter ready and Gloria came out into the yard with Peperoni.

'You're familiar with a martingale?' asked Gloria, as she handed the horse to Sallie.

'Excuse me?'

'Only we thought she might not be, didn't we?' said Gloria, speaking over the top of Sallie's head to Rob.

It was impossible to tell what passed between these two. Sallie immediately wondered whether they were lovers. Anything was possible. She had the powerful and unpleasant sense of having been tricked, or at the very least led into a situation slightly against her will. It had been her own fault, she saw that. There would have been no shame in admitting that, apart from a few lessons at the indoor riding school at Muncie she was in no sense a horse-woman. It was too late to say any of these things now and she had absolutely no idea whether a martingale was a type of horse, a saddle, or just a code word designed to discon-cert visiting Americans.

'We were talking, weren't we,' continued Rob in his gentle burr, 'about whether you'd be used to the old "Western" saddles?'

'A martingale's a saddle?'

At this point the look of agony appeared on Michael's face, then he spluttered with laughter.

'Michael, that's not very nice,' said Frances.

'A martingale's a bridle,' Rob explained. 'Only we wondered whether you'd learnt to ride in a saddle like this' – he was coming towards her with an enormous great hunk of leather, which he extended for her to catch – 'or whether you had the Western ones.'

'I – I – I mean to say I don't . . .'

'You have ridden a horse before?' asked Michael.

The awful thing about this question was that Sallie considered him perfectly entitled to ask it. Rude, humili-ating and cruel, but right. 'Of course,' she said, feeling herself blush.

'I'll let you saddle up,' said Rob.

Peperoni was a huge creature whose glistening flanks touched Sallie's brow. She hurled the saddle on to his back, but he obviously did not like the shock of this and she feared she might have nicked him with the sharp bit of a buckle.

'I'd put the martingale – the bridle – on him first, other-wise . . .' said Gloria. Sallie was humiliated by Michael's laughter; but the expression in Gloria's eyes was actually less forgivable. There was real gloating there.

Gloria helped with the bridle. Why hadn't they told her from the start that the martingale was a stupid bridle?

'I'll leave you to adjust the saddle – you'll want to tighten the girth to suit yourself.'

The girth?

'The girth's the long strap,' said Michael. Potter and Joystick had been ready for some minutes, which already felt like hours. Sallie had the sense that three horses and four people were standing round the yard just staring at her, simply waiting for her to make some ridiculous mistake. They were going to ride out into open country and real fear gripped her. She felt herself perspiring profusely, as she yanked ignorantly at Peperoni's girth. She was facing the animal's tail as she did so, and bent downwards to get a closer look at the buckle. How tight did these things have to be? She pulled the strap one notch tighter and there was a sudden movement from the animal registering discomfort. Sallie was not quick enough to stop the horse turning round and biting her on the bottom.

When she stood up, almost in tears, she felt that they were all holding back laughter. It would have been better in some ways if they had just laughed at her. She could almost have coped with that. It was the politeness with which Michael spoke that really freaked her. 'Ready, now?'

'I think so.'

Gloria no longer was speaking to Sallie as to a responsible grown-up. It was to the children she spoke, as if they were looking after a slightly demented school friend of their own age. 'I think, Mike, for the first time out with Sallie you shouldn't go up Farrer's Copse.'

'I thought we'd go up to Farrer's Copse and then down past the Big Field.'

'Do that another day, Mike, just go down the road and into Big Field from the park end.'

The boy's face screwed into real disappointment. 'Do we have to?'

'Just for the first day out, Mike.'

'It isn't *my* first day,' he said with thinly disguised contempt.

They rode slowly enough down the drive, the horses' feet clopping pleasantly. From the height of Peperoni's saddle, Sallie could see over walls and hedges at the surrounding fields. At once, the delightful knowledge came to her that this was the way to see the English landscape. It was not designed to be seen from human eye level, but from saddle level. At the same time, though the day was bright, the most perfect of early spring days, with a light breeze, she gripped the reins nervously and hoped that they were not going to go any faster than this stately walking pace.

Such was her concentration on the exercise of staying in the saddle and her interest in the surrounding countryside, that she only attended with half an ear to the children, who were speaking to one another.

Everything had changed with Michael's return from school. Frances, who seemed prepared to be Sallie's friend when it was just the two of them, now adopted a noticeably different attitude. She had very distinctly withdrawn a part of herself from the relationship with Sallie. Her closeness to Michael, which was palpable, took the form, as many close relationships do, whether that of siblings or sexual partners, of appearing constantly on the edge of a scrap. He corrected and mocked much of what Frances said, she criticised him for lack of tact or manners. Just

when they appeared to be about to fight, they would laugh
or tease one another, and appear comrades in crime.
Equally, out of a clear sky could come a squall and there
had been a couple of actual quarrels.

'Michael! Gloria said!'

'So *what*? We'll be all right.'

'You and I'll be all right but . . .'

Sallie had not followed the talk between Gloria and
Michael about alternative routes for their ride. It was
evident, though, that they were now diverging from the
agreed route and Frances was hinting as delicately as she
could that, although she was up for it, they could not
expect Sallie to survive the course.

'We'll take it gently,' the boy was saying.

'But there's a fence.'

'Peperoni can jump that.'

'Peperoni can but . . . '

After a gentle walk along the road, the children had
directed their ponies through a gap in the hedgerow and
they had moved into a field that sloped gently upwards
towards a little copse.

'Michael, we must go gently.'

'When did you last ride?' the boy asked, and Sallie was
aware of being addressed.

'I haven't ridden this year – since I came to England.'

'We can either just go up to the top of that hill, or we
could ride up to the hill, down the other side, over these
really, really easy jumps . . .'

'Michael, there's a hedge and a stream,' protested Frances.

'Let's see how we go,' said Michael.

He either did not hear, or chose not to hear, Sallie when
she called out that she thought that they should obey
Gloria's directions.

'It's no fun if you can't gallop a bit' were the last words she heard the boy speak.

The ponies, as soon as they entered the field, had broken into a trot, so that the children were yards ahead of Sallie and Peperoni. She held the reins very tightly and said, 'Easy, easy boy.' Even as she said the words she wondered where they had come from – a film? Perhaps they had been taught to say this during those tame little mornings during riding lessons in Muncie.

Peperoni did not want things easy. The sight of the ponies, first trotting, then cantering and finally breaking into a gallop up the gently sloping hill, filled him with eagerness to show off his form. He had put his ears back and was making thrusting gestures with his head, which made her fearful of losing the reins. He soon jolted from existence any hope that he'd walk up the hill. Her bottom was still painful from where he had bitten it, but now, as he broke into a trot, the saddle pounded both her buttocks. It was as if she were being spanked by a pair of baseball bats. His breath was fast, his snorts almost sexual. Her desperate whimpers seemed to excite him.

'Oh please, oh please, no!'

Strangely enough, when he actually began to gallop, although it was terrifying, it was easier than some of the earlier, bumpier stages of the ride. This huge, vigorous animal easily sped up the hill and caught up with the children, who had reined in their ponies and were waiting for her near the copse.

Her breath came in jerks as she spoke to them. Once again, Michael's face wore that expression, which could either have been suppressing mirth or pain.

'That was a good run,' she managed to gasp.

'Have you really ridden a horse before?' the boy enquired.

'I'm just maybe a little rusty – not used – England' – and even as the words came forth like sobs, she wondered, 'Why am I having to justify myself to this little *jerk*?'

'No,' he said loftily, 'don't get me wrong, I think you're really awesome – for a beginner.'

Chapter Ten

The neighbours, Artegall by name, issued their invitation some days later. For some reason the strict rule that the children were not to be allowed out of her sight was relaxed in the case of Lucy Artegall, a sensible, pleasant-faced woman in her mid forties. Sallie was shocked to discover how pleased she was at the prospect of a day without Michael and Frances. A glow of happiness suffused her being. She could not remember being so happy, ever.

We speak of leaping at ideas. Both children had literally done this when informed that the Artegalls were to come for the next day to Staverton, and that Frances and Michael would repay the visit the day after. Frances had not been so tactless (as Michael had been) actually to jump for joy, but even she had danced a little.

They maybe just needed a bit of breathing space from one another. That was Sallie's hope. After ten days or so she still felt painfully awkward and shy with them. There was this perpetual feeling that they were holding something back and the painful sense that this something was a joke at her expense.

Excuse me, but have I just said something which is really

stupid? Is it my appearance that bothers you? My voice? She wanted to shout these things at Michael, but of course she knew that this would make things worse. When he provoked her (and she was convinced that he did so deliberately) she tried to keep very, very calm.

It had been mean of the children to patronise her after their riding expedition. Two responses would have been appropriate – either to say nothing about it, or to be grateful that she had been unselfish enough and, God damn it, brave enough to go out riding with them *at all*. Instead it was all that stuff about her being awesome or wicked *for a beginner*. And by the time the incident had been turned into a narrative for Gloria, it was *I don't think she'd ever ridden a hunter before*. Gloria colluded in the patronage with her – 'Good on her for trying' and (which was true but tactless), 'She did very well not to fall off.'

Buttocks and thighs were badly bruised, and for the next two days Rob had taken an hour off to go riding with the children while Sallie stayed behind.

Gloria's willingness to undermine Sallie had been in evidence the day after the ride. Sallie volunteered – Gloria had seemed busy and preoccupied with some work or other in the house – to cook the children's supper. Frances, Michael and Sallie were playing Monopoly and it made obvious sense for her to fix them all some pasta, rather than making Gloria come down from the attic where she'd been tidying.

'Well, if you're really sure,' said Gloria hesitantly, 'it would help hugely. Ken wants me home tonight by half six and . . .'

'Sure I'm sure. We'll just have spaghetti – okay, guys?'

The guys had pronounced it to be fine, and, while the Monopoly game – spread on the oilcloth decorated with ships that covered the kitchen table – was in progress, Sallie put on a large pan of water to boil on the big oven.

While she was at the stove, Michael called, 'Sallie.'

'What is it, Michael?'

The boy's most irritating smile. The one which said, 'You are so dumb, you need things explaining to you in words of one syllable.'

'Sallie, I hope you don't mind me saying this, but you can't build that hotel in the Old Kent Road.'

'Any particular reason?' It was best to keep the tone bright, jokey. 'Don't the residents of the Old Kent Road like hotels? Do I require planning permits to build there?'

'It's just : . . you see' – he shot his sister a sly glance and Frances smiled. 'You haven't built any houses there. And you have to build houses before you can build a hotel.'

'Fine!' There was brittleness in her tone, she could hear it, and her smile felt like it was going to tear the corners of her mouth. 'I'll start at the bottom and work my way up.'

'That is the idea of the game,' he said, slamming the ball back over the net and adding with the sweetest of smiles, 'I hope you don't mind my mentioning it.'

'Why didn't you mention it earlier, when I built my first hotel on Vine?'

'Northumberland Avenue,' said Frances, who automatically corrected inaccuracies whenever she heard them.

'Northumberland Avenue, wherever. I built a hotel there and no one objected.'

'We didn't want to say anything to start with. You hadn't played Monopoly before . . .'

'We didn't want to thrash you,' explained Frances.

So they let her bend the rules; like she was some little kid who needed helping along.

While she fiddled with the spaghetti packet and stared worriedly at the pasta, which seemed to stick together as soon as it was put in the pan, she heard the boy say; 'I never bother with the cheaper areas.' He shook a die and was soon building a couple of hotels on Park Lane.

When the pasta was bubbling, she came back to the table and shot a look at her pile of toy money, next to her heap of cards. She had not counted it before she left the table, so she simply did not know what to make of the suspicion that dawned instantly, that Michael had used some of it to build his hotel empire in Mayfair. Hell, it was a game, who cared. The infuriating thing was that she could not help caring and, after making a poor throw and paying Frances a large rental for landing on one of her railroad stations, Sallie went back to the oven.

The children had asked for their pasta simple. Frances had said she liked to stir butter into hers and she'd then add cheese. Michael said he did not want anything, nothing at all, on his spaghetti. But when she'd drained it Sallie thought it looked pretty boring. Rummaging in the fridge, she found a jar of Pesto, which must mean someone around this place ate it? She stirred the green sludge into the pasta, savouring the oily, basilly aroma that rose in the steam. Then she put the pan on a mat at the far end of the table, and came back with a grater and two sorts of cheese, Cheddar and Parmesan.

This was the moment Gloria chose to come back down from whatever she'd been doing upstairs. 'That smells nice,' she said, with a knowing little smile.

The little girl took the food passively and grated some cheese on to her spaghetti.

Michael's stricken expression now seemed much closer to tears than mockery. 'I'm sorry, I said just plain.'

Gloria should have let Sallie deal with this one alone, but she immediately butted in with, 'Try just a bit, Mike – now Sallie's made you some.'

Sallie filled her own plate with spaghetti. 'It's good,' she said – more aggressively than she'd meant. 'Try some.'

'It's very nice,' said Frances, but she was only picking at her food.

'You're not expecting me to boil up a whole new pan of spaghetti with no sauce?' asked Sallie.

'It's fine,' said Michael with a little martyr's smile.

'You'll be hungry if you don't eat.'

'I'll be fine.'

She wanted to take the pan of spaghetti and empty it over his head. There was a pronged spaghetti spoon for serving. She wanted to hammer it repeatedly into his arrogant face.

'Excuse me a moment,' she said.

In the downstairs toilet she filled a basin with cold water and splashed her face. He's only a kid. Nothing matters. Cool it.

She did not know how long she was gone. Upon her return, she could smell fish. Gloria had moved in, and was preparing fish fingers with tomato ketchup and oven chips for both the children.

'Kids!' she said brazenly. In spite of the mock exasperation in her voice, Gloria looked actually triumphant that the children had not eaten the food prepared by Sallie. 'Not worth arguing with 'em. Life's too short.'

There were many things Sallie wanted to say in reply to this. She suppressed them and asked brightly, 'Shall we go on with Monopoly?'

It was while the children ate their fish fingers, and Gloria ladled the remains of the spaghetti into the trash can, that

the telephone rang – and it was Mrs Artegall who tele-
phoned.

'I should think they'd love it,' Gloria was saying into her
mobile. 'Play tomorrow with Freya and Oliver?'

That was when they had jumped for joy.

So now, a whole free day, from ten till six, stretched
ahead. Sallie half thought that it might be a good idea to
go up to London, spend a few hours in the British Library,
maybe even try to meet up with Kate, whose bright idea
it had been that she should seek nannying work. Much as
she wanted, however, to get away from Staverton, she also
wanted to savour it as a grown-up, to enjoy it calmly
without the egotistical omnipresence of the two children.

Jakie Kenner had been in her care for sometimes four
or five hours at a stretch, but his mother always came
home in the evening and Sallie could go back to her own
bedroom, her own television, her own mom's cooking. She
had never supposed, when she had sat in Charles Masters's
office being interviewed for this job, how full full-time is.
She could not have predicted how completely she would
have to pander to the whims of others. Maybe the job was
what she chose to make of it and she was doing it all wrong?
A talk with Kate would have helped here. A more assertive
person would have been able to make herself the children's
acknowledged leader without overt bossiness. She could
have been more imaginative about how they spent their
time. Very many of their waking hours had been spent, the
three of them, hunched in front of a television on a large
landing near their bedrooms, where there was a sofa, a low-
slung armchair and a library of excruciatingly boring videos.
Even when they weren't really watching these videos, the
children used the fact that the television was on as an excuse
to ignore Sallie. What else was there to do? The riding

expedition did not look like being repeated. Michael said the trampoline was kids' stuff. Michael had pointedly shown her his collection of fishing rods, which he identified for use 'when Daddy came'. He had asked her if she fished and seemed from his smirk to add this activity to the list (it included cricket) of things she could or would not do.

She just wished there were not this feeling always that everything was her fault. She blamed herself and felt the others blaming her, Michael, Frances, Gloria. Was the difficulty that the children sensed she was unlike the previous nannies? Did they sniff out the fact that she had come to Staverton, not to look after them so much as to marry their daddy? If this was not absolutely the case, it was the closest thing to the truth that she was able to see. And it was surely this that prompted her, as the future mistress of Staverton, to spend the day here alone, while the children, clutching towels and swimsuits (for the Artegalls had a heated pool) had piled cheerfully shrieking into the back of the large Volvo hatchback.

She had told Gloria not to bother about preparing even the most rudimentary lunch. Sallie said she would forage in the fridge, eat an apple, take a bit of cheese. She wanted, in the few blissful hours to herself, to reread the James novella, bringing to it the thoughts she had been having since she came to Staverton and the impressions that had been surfacing from the deeps during the many hours when she had been too tired or too busy to study.

Refreshed by solitude and a snack, Sallie walked the parterre in midday sunshine. She was still aching from the ride; but the hour or two of reading had given her the need for a mental, as well as physical, stretching of the legs. The reread had been, not in her dog-eared paperback, covered with pencilled notes and cluttered with the modern business of an introduction by a famous, explanatory end-notes by a lesser, scholar. Instead, she had read *The Turn of the Screw* in Charles Masters's handsome old blue cloth-bound library edition, with its hot-metal printing, its thick paper, its title pricked in gold on the spine, and this had enabled her to be carried by the narrative alone without pausing to share the observations and elucidations of the commentators.

Something that had occurred in the library was a revival of her *fear* when she read the story. She had now read it so often, and dwelt so much upon the rival theories and interpretations in the secondary literature, that she had begun to take for granted, hence to forget, the simple fact that it was meant, in the words of one of the gentlemen gathered round the fireside at the beginning of the text, to be 'a scare'. They are gathered round a fire at Christmas telling stories calculated to make the hairs on their necks rise. A story has just been told about a ghost appearing to a child, just one child. And it is now that Douglas produces his story of two ghosts appearing to two children.

'If the child gives the effect of another turn of the screw what do you say to two children –?'

'We say, of course,' somebody exclaimed, 'that they give two turns!'

These listeners, and by extension the readers, are on the lookout for thrills. *The Turn of the Screw* ups the ante. But being dealt with here is something truly nasty and part of the nastiness – Sallie had not appreciated it before – is this very setting of an old country house at Christmas and the men gathered round to taste horror for gratification. This time round, as she began to read, she had wondered whether the story could not be seen as a paradigm of child abuse. Did not paedophile men gather round like-minded individuals to share their cheap thrills? Now, they could do it on the Internet rather than in cosy circles round firesides. And they were wanting just what Henry James in this story is able to supply, some angelical little infants, who can be seen to have dabbled in unspeakable evil and are then cleansed by death! Henry James in the chat room!

There could be no doubt in her mind, as she read, that *Turn* reveals, as do his more heavily populated and extended novels *What Maisie Knew* and *The Awkward Age*, an obsession with childhood innocence being brought face to face with adult sexuality. The abhorrence always expressed at the confrontation surely borders upon a fascination. And there can be no doubt that what horrifies the governess, who is telling the story of *The Turn of the Screw*, is that her charges, who seem so innocent, as well as so beautiful, have secretly been corrupted by Peter Quint, the valet, and that this corruption had been abetted by Miss Jessel, the governess.

Lurid stories in which adults get together to torture, or molest, or even to kill a child were part of the journalistic subculture. Sallie had already, from her short time in England, discovered British equivalents to these Grimm's tales monsters, found in the cheaper American papers, the more sensational TV stations. It was always worse when a woman was involved, either perpetrating the sexual violence or simply colluding in her lover's wish to do so.

James allows the mind to supply absolutely the lowest depth of corruption because he never specifies what exactly has gone on between the children and the abominable spirits. Quint has so corrupted little Miles that the school asks the child to leave. The worst that is hinted at in the story is that this beautiful boy has used bad language, and possibly that he has stolen letters at school, as he later steals the governess's letter, written to her employer to warn him of the strange goings-on at Bly. A modern version of the story, Sallie noted grimly, would almost certainly contain overt reference to sexual dealings between the man and the little boy, possibly involving the girl and Miss Jessel.

Part of James's cleverness is precisely in not saying what has corrupted the children, nor spelling out how this corruption manifests itself. It leaves the apparitions themselves, who are always silent, so much more terrifying. Sallie had found, in the library, that she had been truly alarmed, physically shaken, by the first appearance of Peter Quint to the governess. The young woman in the story was walking in the garden when she looked up and saw him, peering down at her from one of the towers. The next appearance had been even more terrifying, when Quint's pale sinister face appeared at the dining-room window. At that stage she did not know it was a ghost and it was only by questioning the old housekeeper, Mrs Grose, that she realised what she had seen had been the master's former valet.

'Yes. Mr Quint is dead.'

Yet for Sallie the most frightening appearance of all had been that of the former governess, Miss Jessel. The narrator had taken little Flora down to the lake on a hot afternoon. Since they had been studying geography together they whimsically make the ornamental water into the Sea of Azov. Several of the critics in Sallie's notebooks had made much of the fact that innocent little Flora had picked up a flat piece of wood with a hole in it and was trying to thrust a stick into the hole to make a mast. Sallie duly noted that this was what they thought, though, with her absolute dread of that activity, her disgust at the very words used – to the point that she would avoid using the word penetrate in a non-sexual sense – she had tried to discount what these truly filthy-minded critics had seen. Surely – she felt it even more strongly having just reread the story – what is frightening about the incident of Flora by the lake is something that has nothing to do with sexual innuendo.

The horror derives from two brilliant devices. The first is that the governess, in her fear, can hardly bring herself to face 'what I had to face', as she puts it. And so it is only in the following chapter, when she is relating the incident to old Mrs Grose, that we are told precisely what, or rather precisely whom, she has seen. We learn that she has seen a woman.

The second horror is that little Flora had seen the ghost and been entirely unfrightened by it.

'Flora saw!'
Mrs Grose took it as she might have taken a blow in the stomach. 'She has told you?' she panted.
'Not a word – that's the horror. She kept it to herself! The child of eight, *that* child! Unutterable still for me was the stupefaction of it.'
Mrs Grose, of course, could only gape the wider. 'Then how do you know?'
'I, I was there – I saw with my eyes: saw she was perfectly aware.'
'Do you mean of *him*?'
'No – of *her*.'

There follows the description of the former governess's ghost: 'a figure . . . of unmistakable horror and evil: a woman in black, pale and dreadful – with such an air also, and such a face!'

The ghosts are frightening enough, but what hit the pit of Sallie's stomach that morning, as it had done the stomach of the good old housekeeper at Bly in the story, was that the little girl knew all about the ghost and was perfectly happy in the apparition's presence.

Later, as the story advances and the narrator comes to believe that the children truly are in league with the spirits and holding secret conversations with them, the reader enters that deep part of James's imagination where super-natural horror and infantile sexuality collide.

Such a powerful reading experience necessitated a break, a garden walk. She knew, even as she set out on her explor-ation, that her choice of exercise was in such highly charged imaginative circumstances emotionally suggestive. Already, in letters and e-mails to Lorrie she had made references to the similarities between Staverton and Bly. Lorrie, in her last, had expressed the hope that Sallie would not meet Mr Quint in the grounds.

The parterre at Staverton ends with a flight of steps leading through high yew hedges into an enclosed formal garden. Sallie was hoping to retrace the walk she had enjoyed with Frances on her first day at Staverton, in which it was possible to complete a long circle without retracing one's steps. She seemed to recollect that this would involve going through the shrubbery, entering the kitchen gardens, enclosed with high brick walls, turning left beyond some greenhouses and then returning to the house from its western side . . . But it was all very confusing.

Turning back for a moment, as she approached the *allée* between the yews, she looked up at the large red-brick house. She had begun to derive pleasure, when out in the garden, from trying to identify the windows in the upper storeys. Her own bedroom she had actually marked by hanging a small coloured hand towel from the casement. On a lower storey, dead centre and above the library windows, was *his* room, the place where she slept and to which she had come to refer in her mind as *our room.*

She had never felt so strongly, as she did during this particular walk, that she was destined to stay at Staverton for a very long time, perhaps for ever; to become its, and hence Charles's, mistress.

The word, of course, had its connotations, one of which worried her in the nights when she lay in his bed. She had decided that he was a good man, a kind one. He had his two children. There was absolutely no need, ever, for him to do that thing again, to make more babies come. There could be holding, and cuddling, and even petting. This would be enough to assure him that she was, indeed, the mistress of Staverton.

A mysterious sense of belonging, the feeling that all this was, truly, hers, came over her as she turned from the large brick house and continued her exploration of the garden. At the end of a gravel path there was a small slope and it was down this that she distinctly remembered Frances scampering, that first day when the little child had welcomed her – in those sweet, good days before Master Poison came back from school.

Having herself scampered in the same direction, Sallie then found herself at a loss. Left, past some bushes, or . . . Her thoughts about *Turn* had been so powerful, and so detailed, that she had not been concentrating on where she was going; and the equal distraction of sensing this garden, with its limitless lawns and trees, was in some senses already hers had provided no built-in sense of where, in her newly acquired domains, she actually was. An exact retracing of her first walk with Frances was not going to be possible. She was a little bit lost. This did not matter. She would press on, enjoying her thoughts, sometimes about her future life in this place with Charles and sometimes wrestling with *Turn* problems. Rather than taking the scenic route on which the child had led her she had, in fact, turned back on herself and found herself faced with the choice of going round to the front of the house, or walking round some sheds which abutted the stables.

She had taken a dead end. Turning back from the sheds, she saw yet another door in yet another brick wall, unable to remember whether or not she had been here before. The door was open and, framed in its arch, there stood a red-haired woman. It was not Gloria. She was shorter than Gloria and younger, about forty. She had neatly bobbed hair, a black sweater and black trousers. Her face was totally white. It had no colour in it at all. She was staring intently, but at the same time vacantly, in Sallie's direction. Though Sallie tried to look back at her, their eyes never met. Sallie felt she was staring into nothingness.

But there she was.

Staverton was so vast, and so confusing, that there would have been nothing so remarkable about coming upon a figure whom she had not seen before. Had she been in a mood to consider the matter rationally, she might have recognised that there could well be people who came in now and again to help with the garden or the stables. But the disconcerting thing about the woman in black was that she was familiar. Sallie knew her. She had seen her face every night before she went to sleep for the last ten days. This was Charles Masters's dead wife.

As the recognition dawned, Sallie felt herself dehydrating. Her heart hammered inside her chest. Her mouth opened and shut as if gasping for breath, or drink, and she found herself clasping her face as she trembled and whimpered. Then at last they came, from the bottom of her guts, the air-rending screams.

Chapter Eleven

No one came. Not at first. That, for Sallie, was a thing in retrospect which defined Staverton. A human being could scream (for several minutes? How do you time your own screams?) and no one would necessarily hear you. Or they'd hear you, but maybe finish off whatever it was they were doing before they came running.

Certainly this had been Gloria's approach. By the time she found Sallie, still rooted to the same spot on the gravel path, the screaming had stopped.

'Oh, Sallie, hello. Did you hear some awful hullabaloo?'

'Oh, oh.' Sallie was too incoherent to reply. She was shaking, not weeping exactly but in a state very near to tears.

'Only Ted's just rung from the workshop, rung on my mobile, said he heard a scream or something. We do get ramblers coming across the estate and they have been known to come into the garden. You can't be too careful, even if the kids are out of the way today.'

'I . . . I . . .'

'Women being dragged in the bushes and raped. Ken and I sat up and watched *Crimewatch* last night. Terrible thing, a young woman just walking back from the station. This bloke come at her from behind, out of nowhere she said it seemed. Only you saw nothing?'

'I'm sorry, Gloria, I'm sorry, I was . . . I . . .'

'Like a pig being slit, Ted said it was. Look, you haven't met Jill's husband Ted yet, have you. Both the sort to keep yourself to yourself.'

A pot-bellied man of about fifty emerged from one of the sheds. He wore an oily overall and his hands were blackened with grease. He smelt of tobacco and his teeth were dirty. His face was ruddy, plump, peasanty. His hairstyle was a 1950s advertisement for Brylcreem. But he could have been one of the rougher types on Chaucer's Canterbury pilgrimage.

'This is Sallie, who's come to look after the kids for a bit.'

Ted was one of those English people who laughed at everything even when it wasn't funny. 'That'll keep you busy, then.' He chuckled.

'Just for a bit,' Gloria emphasised.

'Well, there've been plenty who's done that job,' he said with another chuckle. 'No, I thought someone were killing a pig. I thought fucking hell, has old Rob brought home the bacon for the first time in his life?' More laughter. 'It were a real screeching noise. Loud as a peacock. But do you know, *it might have been a bird*?'

'I didn't hear anything in the house,' said Gloria. 'You didn't hear anything?'

Sallie realised she was being addressed.

'If there'd *been* peacocks,' said Ted, momentarily serious, 'I'd have said it was peacocks. But dear, oh dear, I thought what can that almighty row be all about? Only you never know. That's why I rang you, Gloria.'

'You were right,' said Gloria. 'There could have been something. Well, if you didn't hear anything, Sallie, and there's no obvious victim of the crime as you might say . . .'

Ted showed Sallie his grimy fingers and explained, with belated courtliness, 'Only, I won't shake hands. You can see – I was in the shed taking a tractor to pieces when I heard it.'

'All's well that ends well,' said Gloria brightly.

'Look, Gloria, now I've got you. If Charles rings back.'

Sallie had been listening to their exchanges with only half an ear. It seemed so extraordinary to her that they did not realise the screams had emanated from her. And now he spoke to Gloria of Charles's telephone messages as if they were a frequent occurrence and she felt very much excluded. How could he ring often and not ask to speak to her?

Ted had switched off the banter and was now speaking with great vigour. 'Tell him I can buy the parts *if he wants me to*. It's gonna cost him.' At the thought of the money being expended, Ted's lips became very stiff. 'I mean, he's in a bad old way, that tractor.'

'Oh, Charles knows that. The question is whether it's throwing good money after bad. I mean, if you can get it up and running, Ted, then the parts is going to cost less than the price of a new tractor. Let's face it.'

'So long as 'e knows,' said Ted, rubbing his trousers with the oily hand. He turned back to Sallie, perhaps aware of her feeling left out. 'I won't, as I say, shake hands – a bit oily.'

'That's quite all right,' said Sallie. She could still hear the tremble in her voice. The disagreeable thought occurred that they could hear it too and were studiedly ignoring her distress.

'And you were standing right there and didn't hear a thing,' he said again, referring to the screech. 'Anyway, Gloria, my love, I'm sorry I bothered you. Only, I could have sworn . . . This place is so deserted. You'll find it lonely I shouldn't wonder?' The serious subject of money abandoned, and the possibility of a visitor being unhappy considered, Ted's manner brightened. He was positively cheerful as he put the question.

'Yes, I do, as a matter of fact,' said Sallie. 'I find it very lonely.'

'All on your own here with the kids?'

'That's right.'

'My missis wouldn't do it. Gloria asked Jill once, do you remember? When you and Ken were wanting to go on holiday? *I'm not sleeping in that house.* Emphatic, my missis was. Most emphatic.'

'It's during the day I get lonely,' said Sallie.

'Sleep the night?' he repeated. 'In that dirty great place? Oh well, I must be getting on.'

When he had turned back to the sheds, Gloria unnecessarily explained, 'There's a perfectly good garage in Lymingbourne; but he's a jack of all trades, Ted. Doesn't like spending money, and if he can fix a car or a tractor himself without VAT and all that palaver . . . We couldn't keep the gardens even half as straight as we do without Ted. Ted and Rob – that's all we have really, and Buggins.'

While she once again speculated on the likely identity of this third member of the team, Sallie realised that Gloria was focusing attention on her.

'Look, are you all right?'

Sallie had begun to cry.

Gloria took her back to the house, flicked the kettle for an instant coffee. She had done so with a briskness that suggested she had more important things to do. Sallie felt that once they had been through the formulae of a few comforting words, Gloria would thankfully resume her morning's chores; she even wondered whether there always reached a point, with the temporary nannies, when for one reason or another they started screaming.

'It's bound to seem strange here,' Gloria said. 'You're bound to be a bit lonely. But you know, we are trying to be your friend.'

'I thought I saw . . . I thought . . .'

'As I say, we get ramblers coming in the garden, we get some very funny types. I've been frightened myself at times.'

This observation made it clear that Gloria realised Sallie was the one who had screamed. What Sallie could not bring herself to say was 'I have just seen the ghost of Charles's dead wife'. Already, as she had allowed herself to be led back to the kitchen, she felt more like a child with a scraped knee than a grown-up who had undergone a profound trauma. If she attempted to say what she had seen, Gloria would have dismissed the story as madness. Perhaps it was madness? During one of the phases of life when she had sought help, a therapist had once told Sallie that we exhibit bizarre behaviour patterns not because one sort of behaviour is 'sane' and another 'abnormal'. It is rather that we want people to notice us, to cosset us, to love us.

The therapist had been one of the regular counsellors at Bethany, the clinic on campus at Carver. It was not the psychiatrist whom she had seen after the incident with Jakie in the bath. This had been when, after a period of depression, she had lashed out at a grad in her dorm. Kimberley Markevich. Mark a Bitch. Kimberley, as well as being the most irritating member of her dorm, messy, loud, flamboyant, was also attending the same classes as Sallie – the Henry James classes, as it happened. She'd made some smart-ass remark during one of these classes, which absolutely cut across something Sallie had been trying to say about James and hyperreality. Bitch. Mark the Bitch. By the time Kimberley had had her say, the professor had moved on and Sallie's much cleverer and more interesting point had been lost, left in the air. Later, in the dorm, Sallie had found the washing machine in the basement full of Kimberley's clothes. That made her really mad. They were just lying there and they had not been washed, they hadn't been spun, they hadn't been dried. She knew they were Kimberley's, anyone would know that pink T-shirt, which stopped above the navel and her pot belly, and those silly purple socks. Sallie, finding these clothes, had overcome her disgust, reached into the machine and thrown them all over the floor.

'Would you mind explaining just what you're doing?'

It had been Kimberley's voice, of course. She'd been watching Sallie all along. 'I was just about to wash those clothes and there you are throwing them all over . . .'

She had not managed to finish that sentence. Sallie had picked up an electric iron, which lay on a ledge in the laundry room. It had not been switched on recently, so it wasn't hot. Otherwise she would indeed have Marked the Bitch Markevich. There was blood again that time, but someone, one of the big sophomores who lived on Kimberley's floor, had done filthy things with her too no doubt, happened to be coming into the laundry and grabbed Sallie from behind.

Kimberley had not pressed charges – no more had Mrs Kenner. A course of therapy was recommended. Kimberley's face was badly gashed. She had been hit by the sharp end of the iron and it had dented a brow and nearly gouged out an eye.

'You think', the therapist had said, 'that you did that because you were just angry with Kimberley. But no one is just angry, Sallie. What you wanted was to be noticed, to be loved. We get mad – and that's what we are, mad, crazy. Doing things which will make people say, "Hey, there's Sallie!"'

There'd been some crazy stuff from that particular therapist about Sallie wanting that great hunk of a football player to come along and grab her from behind. That was really crazy. But maybe there was something about these crazy moments – hitting Kimberley with the iron, screaming at the sight of a ghost – as being cries for help?

Why was she thinking of Kimberley, while Gloria spoke, and while, with automatic movements, she stirred her instant coffee and drank as quickly as she could? The Kimberley incident was closed. Like the Jakie one. And like the few, very few, other occasions when she had lost it, flipped, shown a little behavioural disturbance, like anyone might. (In that category, by the way, she very definitely did not include the pummelling she gave to Hugh, the New Zealand metallurgist, when he had tried to change their smooching into something filthy. That was simple self-protection, and he'd been scared shitless she might bring an attempted rape charge and so lose him his scholarship.)

'Only as I say, we do get strangers wandering around the place,' said Gloria. 'One come walking across the lawn the other week when I was here on my own – Frannie was at school and Mike was away, of course, and I thought oh my GOD what are you thinking of? He was harmless. I called out of the window, "Can I help?" He went on his way rejoicing as you might say.'

'Gloria, I have just seen a ghost. The ghost of Charles's dead wife. She came to me and I can tell you why. She is jealous of me. She thinks I am going to marry Charles when he comes back from Hong Kong.' It was all so simple. But Sallie could not bring herself to say these simple, explanatory words to Gloria. She felt herself, as she sipped her disgusting coffee and made the appropriately grateful little grunts in reply to Gloria's patronising remarks, as being seen by the English giantess as a neurotic little thing. She tried, as Gloria repeated that if she felt lonely she had only to call on her, not to think that there was something about Gloria, something in the way she moved her head, which reminded her of Kimberley Markevich.

'What was Charles's wife called?' she blurted out.

Gloria looked shocked. 'She's called Rosie,' was the answer.

Upstairs, later, in her room, Sallie stared at herself in the bedroom mirror. Her bedroom – not their bedroom, the bedroom she shared with Charles. Her very pale face had lately become oily through stress and was developing a few unbecoming pimples. She blamed Michael's supercilious manner for each and every one of these shining red advertisements of her unhappiness. Squeezing one that wasn't ready to be squeezed, she made it worse, turning what had been a slightly sore pink mound into a scarlet contusion. She had been holding her flesh much too tightly, just because it made her so mad to think of zits at her age, and just because of a kid!

She took in a deep breath and tried to think through the experience of the last few hours calmly. Be rational, Sallie. Maybe you are going crazy. Maybe, after all you've been through you are going, just a little, crazy. In this place, would it be surprising? Look, for the last year you have done very little with your life except read *Turn*, study *Turn*, figure out different ways of saying something new about *Turn*. And this morning, you read it through again, from the moment when she falls in love with her employer to the moment that little boy falls back dead in her arms.

Oh, no, sir. She did not do it. That little heart stopped beating all on its own. No one could point to her.

Her conversation, that one and only conversation, with Charles Masters had been more crammed with double meanings, damn it, than a Henry James short story. There had been just so many suggestions that could not be spoken; so many promises that could not be quite voiced; so many proposals that had to be encoded. That had been her last conversation. Her last real conversation with a grown-up. She did not count Gloria's chats as conversation.

Before that conversation – *the* conversation – with Charles Masters had stretched the weeks and weeks during which she had hardly spoken to anyone.

Sallie leant forward into the mirror. She looked very closely at her own eyes, their quivering liquid sclerotic, slightly bloodshot, the hazel-coloured irises, their surfaces kaleidoscopes of tiny and variegated particles, greenish grey, gold and brown. Closer and closer she stared at her own eyes, staring at the depths of the large distended pupils. Reliable, damn it. These eyes had seen – *Her*. Sitting there, Sallie knew that her eyes had not deceived her. She felt a wave of relief that she had not told Ted or Gloria about her experience. They'd have exchanged those glances, those silent conspiratorial looks, and concluded she was a nut. She knew she was no nut. But could she be sure, completely sure, that the experience had not suggested itself – because she had been reading *Turn*?

Yet she had seen her.

By the time Lucy Artegall brought the children home, Sallie had calmed down. With a careful approximation of English brittleness, Sallie blurted the hope that the Artegalls would all come in, have tea.

'We'd better not – left a frantic au pair with a yammering two-year-old, and an equally yammering husband gets into Lymingbourne on the six thirty-four. But look – next time, you come too? They were super – as always!'

This compliment was accepted by Michael and Frances. Sallie found their forms of politesse hard to come to terms with. She liked to think of herself as a person with manners and in general she thought most Americans, including kids, had much better manners than the English. Michael and Frances, though, had these forms of courtesy which were like acting. There was gush in Michael's 'Thank you *so much*, Lucy'.

'Yes, *thanks*,' Frances gushed too.

'You must all come over here one day,' said Sallie. 'We could play tennis, have some fun.'

Michael and Frances exchanged one of their annoying glances.

'My dears, love to, but must love you and leave you – till very soon!'

Lucy Artegall had a kinder face than Gloria. She was, at least, a woman. Sallie admired her skin, her hair, her air of good health and of pleasantness. Sallie felt that if only she could persuade Lucy to stay for five minutes, they might become friends. 'Please stay!'

'You're so kind!' was Lucy's farewell.

None of them knew what she had seen, nor what she was going through. So their breeziness felt like callousness: the children's non-committal remarks about their day at the Artegalls'; Gloria's bluff no-nonsense manner as she put a large shepherd's pie on the kitchen table and, when it was eaten and the meal cleared away, left.

None of them could know, and none of them would understand if she told them.

The shepherd's pie was extremely good. Michael plastered his plate with ketchup and ate with greedy slurps.

'Didn't Lucy feed you, then?' asked Gloria.

Between mouthfuls he looked up, showed the grin which was between agony and satire.

Frances never commented on her brother's fussy eating habits, but it could be assumed that he had rejected whatever was placed before him at the Artegalls'. It was his way of forming a bond with Gloria, Sallie decided – he'd only eat Gloria's cooking.

When the ketchup splurged on to the pie cooked by Gloria, Sallie saw the sharp end of the iron colliding with Kimberley's eye and brow; saw the red ooze rip skin, moisten hair.

'You're not eating much,' said Gloria.

You're not worth talking to, said Sallie's silent eyes. Lucy, though. She was a woman. She would understand. Lucy had known *Her*? Known Charles and Her together before the children came? She must get to know Lucy. She must make Lucy like her. Maybe she could ask to borrow some of Lucy's clothes, in a kind of girly, friendly way?

'Why don't we make a date for the Artegalls to come over here and play?' she asked.

'I dare say Lucy wouldn't mind dumping the older kids on you – give her an hour or so of peace,' said Gloria.

That was not what Sallie had meant at all.

'I could arrange that for you if you feel up to it,' Gloria added.

Thank you, I can call Lucy Artegall on my own, thank you very much, said Sallie's silent eyes as the anger rose.

It was a relief when no one mentioned a board game for that evening. She could not have faced Monopoly, and Trivial Pursuit with Michael just became an excuse (what was there which did not?) for him to show off. They quarrelled about the rival merits of *Lord of the Rings* and *Harry Potter*, but once the DVD was in the machine they watched more or less silently until it was nine o'clock, barely even noticing as Gloria put her head round the door and told them she was setting the alarm.

Since the children had showered after their swim *chez* Artegall, there was no need for them to do more than clean their teeth and put on pyjamas.

Only very much later, days later, did she look back on that evening and wonder whether there had been something conspiratorial about the children's compliance, their willingness to go to bed at nine, before the film was over, their lack of talkativeness. An hour or so later, when they should by rights have been asleep, she could still hear the murmur from Frances's room. At the time, though, she thought nothing of it. If two lonely kids wanted to go to one another's rooms, to talk late at night, what of it? She was being paid to look after them, not be their gaoler.

And she needed, oh, she needed so badly, to get back to Charles's room, their room, to check the impressions of the day against the photograph in the frame. As the hours had passed, she had come to a calmer frame of mind and to a reasonable conclusion. She had indeed been reading too much Henry James and she had put two things together: her obsession with a story of ghosts returning to a large old house where only a governess and two children might see them; and her own obsession with Charles and his dead wife. When she saw a red-headed Englishwoman in a black turtleneck and black trousers, she had made this woman into Rosie Masters. She had seen her for only a few seconds before the impression was formed, then something broke inside her and she had started screaming. But she had been mistaken. That was the simplest, sanest, best explanation for what had happened.

In spite of the fact that she could still hear the murmuring voices in Frances's room, she could not wait any longer. She set off for her usual nightly resting place. It was not her custom to take anything with her on these occasions. She did not want to leave behind any tell-tale evidence of her presence in his room. And she wanted to put on, not merely his pyjama coat, but the whole of his presence, to wear him like a robe. So she brushed with his hairbrushes and toothbrush, she rolled with his deodorant, she dabbed with his toilet paper.

She also liked, as she lay between his sheets, to fill her mind with the contents of his curiously unnourishing books. They were so hard, so big for her, so impossible to take in.

For the last few nights she had been reading the wartime diaries of Harold Macmillan, who was a British prime minister some time in the 1950s. Did he actually read this stuff for pleasure, Charles? It was fascinating to suppose so, providing a frisson to the mind which was comparable to the sensation of his rough Turkish towels against her poor spotty face, or his badger shaving brush against her bare arms or legs. All the time, in previous evenings, that she had lain there, struggling with Mr Macmillan in Africa, she had felt her gaze, the woman in the photographs. She must be so mad! To sit there in her oh-so-silver frame and see Sallie lying there, in her husband's bed?

Yes, it was your bed once, too? The existence of the children made it impossible for Sallie to sustain the hope, nurtured at first, that they were adopted, that Charles and his wife had not taken part in disgustingness, either in this bed or elsewhere. But there was too much of the photographed woman's face in both the children for such a belief to survive, their red hair, their eyes, their curling lips.

Tonight it was all going to be different. She would know as soon as she saw the photograph whether it had been the woman in the garden.

Chapter Twelve

There could be no doubt. The face staring back at Sallie from its silver frame was the woman she had seen framed by the door in the garden wall. It was the dead woman. As she stared, the full strangeness of it dawned on Sallie.

When she had screamed, it was body and instinct that had wrenched her. Mind had not had time, as it now had, to absorb the thought of what she had seen: a person returned from the dead.

Mom, in Muncie, was a Presbyterian and it was in this religion that Sallie had been raised. She had never been especially religious and so had never had any especially strong anti-religious crisis. In adolescence she had complained about being taken to church; but Mom wasn't a fanatic; she'd only gone every month or so. Of Sallie's high school friends, a couple had been Catholics or Jewish, but most, like herself, came from some kind of Protestant background. Outright atheism had never confronted her until she went to college. Not at Shaker Oakes, where the atmosphere had been of quiet liberal Protestantism. But at Carver some of the professors seemed into all that stuff. One of them had given a class on the crisis of Faith,

Darwin, Herbert Spencer, Freud. She'd taken the class, but it hadn't interested her much. She had not felt the need to give her mind to the questions posed. It was possible to get along without an overall metaphysic, an attitude-to-everything, as opposed to just views about some things which affected you personally. She had not been especially close to either of the two grandparents who had died. Death was not something she had seen at close hand. She had never been forced by crisis to ask herself whether she believed in life after death.

It was, well, it was a Hell's Tone-ish thing to wonder whether Henry James, in constructing a ghost story, had actually believed in the possibility of ghosts. If you wanted your readers to believe in ghosts, you had to, surely? Believe, that is. *Turn* would not have been frightening if everyone – governess, old men at the Christmas party, Henry James, reader – agreed that there could never in any circumstances exist any possibility of surviving death.

Unlike the materialist professor who took the Crisis in Faith course at Carver, Sallie had no underpinning metaphysic to reassure her that the woman she had seen near the sheds could not, in any circumstance, be Charles's dead wife. The rationalists would tell her that her eyes had been deceiving her; or that there had been a woman there, but she had just been someone who bore a surprising resemblance to the woman in the photograph . . . But the rationalists were not being rational. If you knew someone was dead . . . and if you saw them . . . then the rational thing to believe was that this was indeed the person, returned from the dead.

As she lay on the bed, looking at the photograph, Sallie realised that it could not have been a simple hallucination. Had it been just this, then the woman by the sheds would have looked exactly like the photograph. She would have had the same hairstyle, the same clothes, the same jewels, even. The photograph lady had a bare neck and a necklace. The woman by the sheds had a black jumper. The woman in the garden had shorter hair. But there was no doubt. They were the same woman.

And now the question occurred to Sallie: if the woman could appear in the garden, she could surely appear anywhere. She might be here now, in this bedroom, looking at her?

The thought froze Sallie with fear. She did not want to be here. She wanted to be back in her own bedroom, but the thought of the presence in the room made it impossible to move from the bed. She had read stupid stories in the *Inquirer* about poltergeists, spirits that threw furniture about. Needless to say, she had formed mental connections between such examples of modern folklore and the Gothic novels she'd studied in her last year at Shaker. In those early novels of the uncanny, there always turned out to be 'rational' explanations for the ghost. As her professor for the Gothic course said, these stories were entertainments for rationalists. The medieval castle of Otranto, the cloisters of Monk Lewis, the mysteries of Udolpho had not been interesting to the real Middle Ages: they were a phenomenon of the Age of Enlightenment. Yet was not postmodernism, she now wondered, and hence her whole intellectual life in the last four or five years, precisely a reaction against Enlightenment?

Whatever the Enlightenment had to say about ghosts, she was now lying alone, in a house where she was a stranger. She was lying on a four-poster bed, in a shadowy old room, and she was not sure that she could find her way back to her own room in the dark. And she was frightened. Frightened as hell.

And she did not dare to get up because of fear. Even if the Presence in the room was not visible, she had now begun to fear that she might brush against it, or be touched by it. She could envisage something cold, perhaps something clammy, touching her hands or her cheeks, her hair. If, as she now obsessively began to believe, the dead could see us all the time, if they could spy on us, then She, the ghost, had been watching Sallie all these nights in this bed, watching her in the bed that she had once shared with Charles, the bed, perhaps, where she had made these children? Sallie remembered that she had stared with triumph at the photograph, even shown her semi-nakedness to it and taunted it. *At least I am alive.*

With unarticulated, very quiet whimpers, Sallie tried to bargain with the spirit, to apologise for wearing Charles's pyjama coat, for taking his shaving brush to bed, for sleeping on his sheets. Without quite striking a bargain with the Presence, she made some unspoken exchange in her head: if she could get out of the room without being *touched*, she would promise not to return to it. She would leave it to Charles's ghost-wife.

She had swung her legs off the bed and begun to run. She did not care any more about leaving traces of her presence behind her. There would be a time for explanations, or she could go back when it was light to switch off the electric lamp, to tidy the crumpled coverlet. She ran into the corridor and into the darkness and, more by luck than memory, found the bottom of the small staircase leading to her own and the children's quarters.

The landing outside the children's bedrooms was dark and quiet. The murmuring in Frances's room had stopped. It was only when she had regained her own room, with its comforting bright lamps, that she realised there had been something different in the landing corridors. A smell. Her sinuses had absorbed it as she ran along and she could still smell it, so strong was the scent. Sallie did not wear such stuff, nor did Gloria. It was an expensive, exotic smell, like the parfumerie department of the big stores.

She curled on to her bed, only half undressed and slept fitfully with the lamp still lit until dawn appeared at the windows.

Next day, after she had showered and put on fresh clothes, she began to look back with some shame on the experiences of the previous evening. The fears had been caused by the dark; by reading Henry James; by loneliness; by the confusions in her head since her panic attack by the sheds. Under the shower water Sallie told herself that she had imagined the whole thing. Okay, she had seen a woman hanging around the house when the children were away. She had thought the woman looked like the photograph in Charles's bedroom. In the light of day, though, Sallie admitted that those middle-aged, formidable English-women of a certain class looked very much like one another. Dye Lucy Artegall's hair red and she would look more or less the same. Those fears in Charles's room last night had been preposterous.

She remembered then that she had run from his bedroom, leaving the lamp ablaze and the bedclothes crumpled. As soon as she was dressed, Sallie crept along the corridor on the first floor. With the caution of a spy, she looked to right and left. She opened the bedroom door. So she'd shut it the night before?

It was the first time she had seen the room in the pale light of day. The electric lamp beside the bed had been switched off. Through the windows could be seen morning sun touching the bright green tops of trees newly burst into leaf. She could see lawns, and paddock and woodland valley – the best of views, the reason, you saw from here, why some rich merchant in about 1870 had decided to build his house on this spot in the model of a large Elizabethan manor.

Someone had been here before her. The pillows were straight. The red silken bedcover was smooth. It was as if she had herself been a ghost and her tearful, terrified presence on the bed last night had left no physical impression. Sallie sniffed. In the air, she could discern the same expensive scent that had wafted through the darkened corridor outside the children's bedrooms the night before.

Chapter Thirteen

'*Because*, young man. Just because. Never mind why. And because your dad wants Sallie to look after you until he gets . . .'

'Oh, but he's never going to come back from flipping Hong Kong, not before term anyway. He said he'd take us to Rock.'

'He'll take you to Rock next holidays. The weather will be better then – half-term, maybe.'

'Gloria –' it was Frances's voice now. 'We know Daddy's not coming back this holidays because he's stuck in Hong Kong doing his really, really boring work. But all we wonder, Michael and I, is why we have to have Sallie with us every single minute . . .'

'She's spastic . . .'

'Mike, I've told you before not to use that word.'

'Well, she is spastic at tennis.'

'I've asked you all the same. It isn't a nice word to use.'

'Gay, then.'

'I don't know what that should have to do with it.'

'Michael means she's no good at tennis,' glossed the sister. 'Not that she's . . .'

There was indecent merriment.

'She's spaz at Monopoly, spaz at tennis, spaz at riding – she'd obviously never been on a horse before –'

'Like I said, if that's true, all the more credit to her for having a bash.'

'I'd give her a bash.'

It was especially hurtful to hear Frances laughing at this. Sallie had always supposed that Frances at least was her friend.

'Edith was a genius compared with her. Even Nathalie.'

'Nathalie had a moustache.' The little girl tittered.

'Sallie's got a bit of a moustache,' said Michael, as if he'd been thinking quite a lot about the subject. 'Only 'cause she's fair you can't see it as much as you could Nathalie's. And she has spots.'

Sallie crept away from the kitchen door. It was much too late for a theatrical cough to alert them to her approach. As well as hurting her, they had made her extremely angry. She had hoped the children were beginning to like her; God knew, she had put enough effort into trying to make friends. Nothing but contempt was discernible in the way they spoke about her, lumping her together with a string of young women on whom they had been dumped out of school hours. They were not even going to bother to get to know her. They were not going to give her a chance. And they just had no idea, the stupid, *hateful* little creatures, how deep in she already was, not only with their father but with their mother.

Sallie found herself weeping. She could not go into the kitchen and give the little toads the satisfaction of seeing her red eyes. And yet she could not skulk and allow them to continue their odious conversation. She felt she had never known such hatred of human beings. It weakened her, almost to fainting.

Emerging ten minutes later from a downstairs lavatory, she felt she had calmed down. She had bathed her face with cold water and she had tried the deep-breathing exercises which one of the therapists had recommended to her after the incident with Kimberley and the iron.

'Daddy always calls that the Gents,' said Michael's voice through the shadows.

God in heaven, the kid had been watching her, waiting for her to come out of the john!

'I hope that does not mean that females' – surely even this cloth-eared little munchkin could hear the irony which she spread thickly over the word – 'are not entitled to enter it?'

'It's more usual for ladies, well, women, to use their own loos,' he observed brightly. The tone was apparently helpful rather than mischievous, a word to the wise.

As she followed him into the kitchen, he had run ahead and she could hear him reiterating to the others, 'You can see quite clearly it's a Gents: it's got men's clothes brushes on the shelf and a comb and . . .'

'I don't suppose the sky's going to fall in if a lady uses it now and then,' said Gloria. 'Some people don't have more than one loo you know.' It was not possible to judge from her tone whether this was their misfortune (which Michael should pity) or a consequence of lowly station, which he was entitled to despise.

'Ah!' Gloria said in a quite different tone, 'there you are!' There was a strong implication that they had been waiting for hours for Sallie's appearance at the breakfast table. 'Now the others have eaten, I'm afraid. Sausages with eggs, is that what you would like?'

'No, no, really. I'm happy with . . . Maybe just a little yoghurt.'

It was the normally well-mannered Frances who yelped at this.

'Now, we've had enough of that,' said Gloria sharply. Only to upbraid, and hence to notice, was to collude in the mockery.

'I wasn't laughing,' said Frances, going extremely pink.

'If Sallie's having . . . *that*,' said Michael solemnly . . .

While he was putting in a bid to eat Sallie's sausages, his sister was glossing with yoghurt. So that was the joke. They said yoggut and she said yoge-ut. Big deal. You say tomayto and I say tomato, let's call the whole thing off.

'And maybe some toast,' Sallie went on, controlling the rage. She took a breath. Winfred Levin the therapist had been called, on that anger management course after Kimberley. Funny the names stayed with you. 'Maybe a little fruit.'

Since she now knew that she was gay and spastic at tennis, riding and most forms of activity, it required quite a lot of nerve to summon up the next question. 'So – what are we all going to do today? Ask the Artegalls over, maybe? Or why don't we go riding again?'

The boy shot a glance at his sister. It was unmistakably conspiratorial. 'Maybe,' said Michael with his extra-polite smile, 'and it's really, really nice of you, maybe we could ask Oliver and Freya over on Friday. Or maybe next week. I don't know. Today, you see . . .'

'We'd rather stay here today,' said Frances decidedly.

'Well, maybe you'd like an outing.'

'Maybe one day. Today, we'd like to be here.'

'So how 'bout you two helping me improve my tennis?'

Winfred Levin. Strange name for a man. 'Be generous. When you least feel like being generous, give of yourself to the other person, the person you're mad at. Offer them something. Pay them a compliment. You'll find the anger, which is really your feeling of inadequacy towards that person, dying down – because then, you're giving that person something, you're saying, "Hey, I've got something you haven't got!"'

Frances said, 'We are quite happy, you know. This is our home. We don't need entertaining all the time.'

'Maybe not, young lady,' said Gloria, 'but if you're here you're going to need feeding and I'm going to need to know how many, when, how much.'

'It looks like we'll all be in at lunchtime,' said Sallie.

The Winfred Levin technique just did not seem to work with these kids. You offered them something and they just shrugged it off. Sallie consumed fruit and yoghurt in silence, feeling like she'd done as an adolescent when her mother, for no obvious reason, was irritating the hell out of her and she just couldn't control the feelings.

'Just so's I know,' said Gloria.

The children had left the kitchen.

Gloria said, 'You know, Charles does expect whoever's looking after them to supervise them *at all times*. We've had endless trouble with it, as you can imagine. It drives me up the wall when I have to do it, it irritates the kids. The other girls, the ones before you, all come unstuck over it, frankly.'

'Surely,' said Sallie, 'Frances is right – they don't need supervising every minute of every day.'

'Well,' said Gloria. It was a dissenting note, but one which suggested, just for today, that Gloria could not be bothered to lay down the law.

The morning passed quietly. It was perfectly true that the children were old enough to spend a few hours in their own house without supervision. When she had settled herself with her books and her laptop, Sallie tried to take a grip of herself and to remind herself what a difficult situation it was for them. They had no mother. They were missing their father. All kids needed space into which adults did not intrude. Presumably, knowing himself to be an absentee parent who did not see his children enough, Charles felt guilty; and this took the form of his absurd insistence that the supervision of the kids had to be full-time? Or had there been some terrible accident they were keeping from her?

It was certainly warm enough to play outside even if it was not quite warm enough to sit still. Muffled in an anorak and scarf, however, Sallie sat with the laptop on her knees.

It was time, in her thesis work, to go back and ask some very elementary questions about *Turn*. Some of the more abstruse and difficult questions which she had asked in her opening draft chapter, and which had preoccupied so many months at the beginning of her research, had faded in importance. Much simpler questions now demanded an answer.

The first time the governess sees the ghost of her predecessor, Miss Jessel, she forms the instant impression that the ghost is malign. 'The woman's a horror of horrors!' she exclaims to old Mrs Grose, the housekeeper, when recounting Miss Jessel's appearance to her and to the child, Flora.

'"Tell me how you know," my friend simply repeated.' Surely the housekeeper was asking the governess, not simply how she knew it was Miss Jessel, but how she knew that she was wicked?

'Know? By seeing her! By the way she looked.'
'At you, do you mean? So wickedly?'

'Dear me, no – I could have borne that. She gave me never a glance. She only fixed the child.'

Mrs Grose tried to see it. 'Fixed her?'

'Ah! With such awful eyes.'

She stared at mine as if they might have resembled them. 'Do you mean of dislike?'

'God help us, no. Of something much worse.'

'Worse than dislike?' This left her indeed at a loss.

'With a determination – indescribable. With a kind of fury of intention.'

I made her turn pale. 'Intention?'

'To get hold of her.' Mrs Grose – her eyes just lingering on mine – gave a shudder and walked to the window; and while she stood there looking out, I completed my statement. 'That's what Flora knows.'

The baseness and the wickedness were in the *look*. But we are told that Miss Jessel gave the new governess 'never a glance'. She can merely see, or sense, or imagine the wickedness by observing its hypnotic effect over Flora.

The wickedness adds to the effect of horror, naturally. But how could it be discerned so quickly that the woman in black was 'infamous'? What was seen instantly was the rapport between the ghost and the child. The rapport fills the governess with – what? Horror, she says. But surely we see that it is also wistful envy. The little girl is closer to the old governess than to the new.

Such reflections, jotted in note form on the laptop, took the better part of an hour. It was undoubtedly time to go, not to interrupt the children but to keep an eye on them. They had told her that they intended to play tennis. Michael, earlier in the week, had said it was 'no fun' playing the game with someone who was as 'crap' as his sister at the game. Presumably, Sallie reflected bitterly, it was better to play with someone who was crap than one who was both gay and spastic.

When Sallie got to the tennis court, she found it deserted and she realised that she had half expected that this would be the case. She called the children's names, aware as she shouted of how American her voice sounded, especially when calling for the girl.

'Fra—nces! Michael!'

She left the tennis court and came back to the house a different way, close to the sheds where, the previous day, she had seen the apparition. Then some impulse made her turn back on herself and she decided to look in on the large summer house which lay at the end of a grass path between the great yew hedges. It was a summer house which she knew the children used as a playhouse. It was a large Victorian structure, an elaborate version of a Swiss chalet, and Sallie supposed it to be about the same date as the house itself. Because of the way she was approaching it, from the side, rather than headlong down the grass *allée* between the yews, she could not be seen, since its windows only faced to the front. She could hear the children, though, as she approached. Their voices had the happy timbre which had pealed out when they were with Lucy Artegall. Their voices were relaxed, so much at ease that she hesitated to break in upon them, less for their sakes than for her own. Her self-confidence could not quite bear the inevitable stiffening, the abandonment from hilarity, if they knew she was there.

So she crept back the way she had come, round the yew hedge. Then, instead of going back to the sheds and through the stable yard, she strode out towards the lawn and took a path that led towards the terrace. Beneath her, the Kentish landscape was one day further towards summer. The leaves were fuller and greener. In spite of the slight chill, spring was palpably in the air.

Safe at this distance of a hundred yards, she turned back towards the summer house and saw for the first time, through the windows, the children joyfully at play. She could see the excited, happy face of Flora, lit up with merriment. She saw Michael, who was holding cards in his hands. They were definitely playing cards, as they stared, devotedly and fixedly and lovingly at a third figure who sat with them at the table.

Chapter Fourteen

Sallie, your last e-mail scared me shitless. And not for the reason you think. Look, Sal, just go back to London. Please. If you are starting to see ghosts it's time to quit. Sallie, please. Lorrie.

Sallie, of course I am your friend. I just think, from some of the things you say – and from things you don't say – that life might be getting just a little on top of you. That is all. Honestly, I was AMAZED when you told me you were taking a job looking after kids. You told me once that when you'd looked after that kid in Muncie you ended up nearly murdering him! Now you say I made that up, but that was what you said, Sal. At least when you were looking after him you did not see any ghosts. Sal, I had no idea things had gone so far between you and Charles Masters, but now you've told me that, there are some other things I need to talk through with you. Please, Sal, leave now. Go back to London and maybe let's talk. Lorrie.

Sallie, if anyone is being aggressive, it is not me. I assure you! I seriously think you should quit this creepy place right now.

You may think the children are trying to mess things up between you and their father. I'm not sure he's being completely honest with you, Sallie, if he's given you to understand that he is lining you up to be ... did I understand you right, Sallie – to *marry* you? When did this happen? L.

Sallie, I am not trying to undermine you, and no, I have not been in touch with the children, nor with Gloria, whoever she may be. But it's time to come clean with you. I have spoken once to Mr Masters. I am sure he guessed that I wasn't Mrs Kenner. He asked me how many children I had and, Sallie, I'm sorry I said two, and then he said, 'That's odd, Sallie said she only had one child to look after.' Since then, he has left several messages on the answerphone. Sallie, I have gotten so I can't pick up the telephone in case it is Mr Masters. This man is a LAWYER. Sallie, supposing he has started investigating you? Supposing he gets in touch with the faculty at Carver and finds you took that year out at Bethany to get psychiatric help? Sallie, no one is blaming you, but I can't go on lying for you. I have my own career to think of. How's it going to look if I apply for jobs teaching high school and I've told this lie, and covered up for someone who had your difficulty when you looked after Mrs Kenner's little boy? Look, Sallie, just quit. Go back to London. He's not going to pursue you, is he? Nothing's happened yet, has it? I mean you two aren't sleeping together? How can you be? He says in his messages on the telephone that he's in Hong Kong. L.

Sallie, you are right to say I did not even mention the ghosts in my last e-mail. I am sorry, but I do not believe in ghosts, especially when they have been seen by a woman who has not been in grown-up company for a long time, and who has been walled up with two kids, and with nothing to do except read *Turn of the Fucking Screw*. L.

Sallie stared at the screen in impotent rage. It was scarcely credible that Lorrie, who was meant to be her friend, should write to her in this way. Why drag in that stuff about Sallie taking a year out, some of it hospitalised? Sallie hardly knew anyone who had gotten through a university course without undergoing therapy of one sort or another. Lorrie was now trying to make out that Sallie was some kind of nut. And why drag up all that stuff about the Kenner kid, little Jakie? Sallie very much regretted ever telling Lorrie about the incident. She was sure that she had probably exaggerated things a little, to amuse Lorrie. Did Lorrie have no sense of irony? Christ, the kid had fallen against the faucet and cut his head. It was an *accident*.

Sallie now felt she had been really foolish to bring Mrs Kenner's name into the matter. All she should have done was choose the name of some friend – not Lorrie, evidently – and give that to Charles; say she'd done some nannying work for her. Anyone's name would have been enough. It was too late now.

The suspicion occurred that Lorrie was holding quite a lot back. Sallie wondered whether she had not been phoning up Charles Masters, presumably with the pathetic idea that she herself might get off with the man. She had sussed out the fact that Sallie and Charles were at the beginning of something rather more serious than existed between Lorrie

herself and that wimp of a fiancé of hers. At the heart of
many friendships there was envy and spite. Sallie realised
that now. Like, she remembered Lorrie's face when she'd
been told that Sallie had won the scholarship to London.

Lorrie's face had lit up with an artificial smile. 'Oh, come
here! I just want to hug you!' That's what she'd said when
she'd extended the arms of that pale-blue chunky sweater
Sallie had never liked.

What she'd meant was 'Come here, I want to strangle
you!' And behind that, what she'd meant was 'So, what do
you know? Little Sallie Declan! Poor shy little Sallie, the
one who always tagged along with the rest of the Group.
Sallie who had her little troubles and had to spend some
time in the psychiatric hospital. Sallie whose contributions
to the Literary Theory seminar sometimes suggested she
hadn't really understood Lacan. And here she is, our Sallie,
going off to London to do a Ph.D.!'

Wasn't *that* what Lorrie's supercilious smile had hidden?
Friends always hate you when you turn out to be more
successful than they are, more successful than, patronising
bastards that they are, they think you *deserve*. And while
Lorrie stayed behind in Carver, making her tedious wedding
plans with Wilf and wallowing in all the jokes of the Group,
which was, frankly, just a little childish and a little embarrassing, Sallie went off to London. Not only did she live
in Bloomsbury, like Virginia Woolf, and not only was she
doing a doctorate but she had also captured the heart of a
man who owned Staverton! A person like Lorrie, who was
rootedly suburban, could frankly have no conception of a
place like Staverton, its stables, its paddocks, its lawns and
terraces, its estate. Of course a man like Charles asked a
few elementary questions about a woman he had fallen in
love with. Of course he could not stop himself from asking

Lorrie what Sallie was like. But for Lorrie to try to use this against Sallie, to poison the man's mind against her, this was truly evil.

Hitherto, the only things that had stood between her and happiness with Charles had been the children. And the ghost. The jealous ghost. It just made Sallie so angry that Lorrie should now, so crudely, have tried to pitch in.

Sallie had seen the ghost – Rosie. She must learn to call her by her name. To name is to master. She had seen Rosie once alone, by the sheds, and once with the children, in the summer house.

The phenomenon was exactly as described in Henry James's story.

Since coming to Staverton, Sallie had radically revised her thesis and realised that she had been approaching everything from the wrong perspective. The Literary Theory, which she had been struggling to apply to James, was not yielding the light or help she had hoped for. Old Hell's Bells had his points. He had pointed her to the moment of inspiration for *The Turn of the Screw*, to be found in Henry James's *Notebooks*.

Saturday, January 12th, 1895. Note here the ghost-story told me at Addington (evening of Thursday 10th) by the Archbishop of Canterbury: the mere vague, undetailed, faint sketch of it – being all he had been told (very badly and imperfectly), by a lady who had no art of relation, and no clearness: the story of the young children (indefinite number and age) left to the care of the servants in an old country-house, through the death, presumably, of the parents. The servants, wicked and depraved, corrupt and deprave the children; the children are bad, full of evil, to a sinister degree. The servants *die* (the story vague about the way of it) and their apparitions, figures, return to haunt the house *and* children, to whom they seem to beckon, whom they invite and solicit, from across dangerous places, the deep ditch of a sunk fence, etc. – so that the children may destroy themselves, lose themselves by responding, by getting into their power. So long as the children are kept from them, they are not lost: but they try and try and try, these evil presences, to get hold of them. It is a question of the children 'coming over to where they are'. It is all obscure and imperfect, the picture, the story, but there is a suggestion of strangely gruesome effect in it. The story to be told, tolerably obviously – by an outside spectator, observer.

There it was: the outline of *The Turn of the Screw*, including what James had seen immediately, that the story would have to be told not by a novelist third-person narrative, but by an observer of the phenomena. Typically of James, with his obsession with childhood innocence, he makes his *Turn* children (who in the Archbishop's version had been 'bad, full of evil') appear like little angels. Within a page or two little Flora is being likened to Raphael's holy infants and her brother, not yet met, is, according to Mrs Grose the housekeeper, even more of a paragon. 'Oh, miss! If you think well of this one! . . . You will be carried away by the little gentleman.'

Sallie turned off her computer. The light of the screen was making a bad headache worse. She hoped she wasn't coming down with one of the migraines which paralysed her when stressed.

Just supposing that these two kids here at Staverton,

Michael and Frances, had been taken over by an evil spirit, a woman brought back from the dead?

She knew that, spelt out baldly like that, it sounded crazy. That, now she came to think of it, was why Henry James chose to tell his story in the way that he did. And so you get all the smart-asses from Edmund Wilson onwards saying the governess *was* a headcase. Yet it is obvious from the *Notebooks* that as far as James himself was concerned the apparitions of Quint and Miss Jessel are real ghosts and they are evil, with power. James evidently did not believe that it was a sign of insanity to have experienced the paranormal. But he did know that if you failed to tell the story right, it would seem merely absurd. Babyish. She knew now why Hell's Bells had told her to read *Lord Halifax's Ghost Book*, which she had found in the library at Staverton. The comparison was between artless narrations in the popular Edwardian best-seller, which were essentially implausible, and the compelling power of James. *Turn* was true because it was psychologically true and you could read it as a compelling and psychologically terrifying story even if you took the view that ghosts are not real. For these ghosts in some sense were real, all too real.

Sallie tried to review her own situation in comparable terms. She could not tell Gloria that she had seen Rosie's ghost. Sallie even hesitated to use the word ghost when thinking about it. But she could not tell Gloria about Her – It – Rosie. If Lorrie had dismissed the thing as a sign of mental imbalance, what would Gloria say – with her carping desire to find fault with everything that Sallie did or said?

She had seen Gloria's sly glances. She knew that Gloria sided with the kids against her. She knew that Gloria supposed, once the holidays were over, that Sallie would join the line of girls they once had to work at Staverton. How very wrong this was! Sallie looked forward to the expression on Gloria's face when Charles came back from Hong Kong and when the housekeeper was told of the very great changes that were going to happen at Staverton!

But this point could not be reached until Sallie herself had taken things further, worked some things out. She had work to do.

Supposing she had been led to Staverton precisely because her head was full of *Turn of the Screw*? She had been thinking about the old house, and the housekeeper, and the children, and the visitants from beyond for a whole year before she actually needed to confront the reality.

The mind can be prepared for the truly great crises of life by all manner of strange intuitions, intimations and premonitions. Very many people speak of meeting their future husband or wife and knowing instantaneously that they have met the Right Person. It is less a guess than a recognition. 'Oh, so there you are at last.' People have often, very often, come to a place which they know they have not visited in their lives and yet immediately recognised it. It is the place where they are going to live for the rest of their lives.

Human beings are, as it were, prepared for such moments.

What was so crazy about believing that she, Sallie Declan, had been prepared for Staverton, its mellow brick and its mullioned windows, its gardens, its soughing trees, its little children, by the benign old hand of Henry James her compatriot, leading her there, murmuring to her that, before taking Staverton into her possession, she must purge it of its unwanted presences, clean it? Suppose, having gone to Staverton as a childminder, she had in reality been summoned there as an exorcist?

It was essential, this being the case, that she continue to sleep in Charles's bed. It even occurred to her that it was her very boldness in seizing the initiative here, in laying claim to Charles so demonstratively and so obviously, that had wakened the jealous ghost. Maybe if Sallie had not been bold enough, so early, to make the position clear, the ghost would have been content to remain nothing more than just a black-and-white photograph staring fixedly from a silver frame. As it was – well, the phrase which suggested itself to Sallie was that Rosie had returned to put up a fight. She pictured the possibility that she might have to wrestle, quite literally, with the spirit. She remembered the passage in the Bible where the writer of old said that 'we wrestle not with flesh and blood, but against principalities, against powers, against the rulers of the darkness of this world'. It brought into the mind a cluster of associations, of Jacob, wrestling with the angel all night and of not knowing with whom he fought; and other cruder images, fed into the psyche by late-night horror movies on TV, in which a person, usually a young woman, found herself being touched, moved, shaken, wrestled with in the dark.

During the class she'd taken at Shaker on the Gothic Novel, the other students, obsessed by a certain subject, had made so much of supernatural possession being a metaphor for bodily possession. They wanted everything to be a paradigm of that, that most disgusting occupation! But what if such stories were so frightening, and made such a strong appeal, because deep down we all of us believed that we are not just flesh and blood? How about if we all know that we are immortal spirits who will not die when our bodies die? If that inner knowledge is given to all of us, deep and real, what if ghost stories frighten us and make such an impression on us because we believe they are true?

Those presences, those movements, those unseen but seeing eyes, those wraithlike fingers in the dark, they are not a metaphor for anything. They are what we all at a deep level fear. What if the fear is based on a kind of knowledge? Isn't it something absolutely fundamental to us, as human beings, that we somehow know we are immortal?

This was what sharpened Sallie's certainty that Charles's wife was *there*, she had come back, the jealous ghost, in a pathetic attempt to lay claim to her own. It would take courage to face her out, but this was what Sallie would have to do, not only for her own sake but for the kids, too.

Therefore, when the old house became still and the murmur of voices from Frances's room became silent, and her reading for the evening was over, Sallie prepared herself for a night's vigil, exorcism or watch in the room which the jealous ghost was coming back to haunt and reclaim.

She took two more paracetamols and this seemed to be holding her migraine at bay. Nevertheless, her head still throbbed painfully as, carrying her shoes, she tiptoed on tiny stockinged feet down the corridor. She'd done the walk so many times now that she had begun to know the rogue floorboards that creaked, so she skipped and jumped lightly.

It was essential to show Rosie who was mistress of Staverton! This gave her energy. It did not diminish her terror. When she reached their door, hers and Charles's, she realised she had been holding her breath for the entire length of the landing. Now she gasped through an open mouth and could not immediately tell whether the smell, the ghostly odour, Rosie's scent, still lingered. Yet upon entering the darkened room, it seemed as if the scent was there and stronger than ever.

This time she was not going to switch on any lights. In

her first entries and re-entries, her incursions and encroach-
ments, she had a mixture of motives for needing to possess
and command the room. It was hers, of course. Hers and
his. Theirs. But she had also in early explorations felt an
obsessive curiosity, which forced her to rummage through
every sock drawer, every closet, every pillbox in the wall-
mounted bathroom closet, every tie, every shirt. She
needed, then, to hold, or stroke, or lay claim to every bit
so that when in the future weeks and months she saw him
in a particular shirt or a particular pair of undershorts, she
would recognise them as old friends. 'Oh, so you're wearing
that. I know it.' In those early sieges upon his closets she
had also needed to discover what turned out to be so aggra-
vatingly and yet satisfyingly absent, the evidence of other
women: their belongings, their letters. In fact, there was very
little of a personal kind in the room beyond clothes and
some books. There were no diaries and no letters from Rosie.
Light had been required for all those forays. No longer
were fumblings with switches and frantic flashlights needed.
She had entered into spiritual combat. She alone could face
it, and face it in the dark. She simply slipped out of her
jeans and slept in the bed wearing, which she had been
already, one of Charles's shirts, her panties and his shorts
over them, and a pair of his socks.

The room was almost palpably inhabited. Something
said to Sallie that if she could just face it out for one night,
one more night of rivalry and conflict, if she could endure
for just these hours of darkness, the presence of the other
woman, then she could establish that she was now the
mistress of Staverton and the ghost of Rosie would be laid.
This was the logic behind this very necessary, very frightening, course of action. The two girls were going to fight
it out.

The crisp linen sheets were cold to her bare legs. The two lamps beside the bed began, as her eyes accustomed themselves to the dark, to take shape, brooding like heads craned over to peer or to caress. The curtains round the great four-poster shook slightly as if twitched by unseen fingers. And as she snuggled down, waiting for her own body warmth to permeate the bed but in fact feeling colder by the minute, and as she composed herself self-consciously into stillness, she could hear and sense the whole invisible life of the house when left to itself.

Floorboards and window shutters from time to time moaned or gave out stifled murmurs. It was quite believable that, as in the children's stories she had most enjoyed, toys were now coming into life uninhibited by the presence of clumsy childish fingers. Little rodents were perhaps scurrying behind skirting boards and wainscots dressed in bonnets and waistcoats and laced shoes. Beyond the window the night sky was full of stars and wind blew through the numberless trees in the garden and park. Though Sallie watched and waited for one presence, one life form, one life-in-death alone, she was comforted in her fear by a consciousness of innumerable lives of animals and plants and stars and planets filling the night. The dark, though full of terrors, was not full only of terrors. There were also the dormice, the leaves, the moon. Night brought its reminder that her awareness of life in daylight, her visual impressions, only formed a small part of her awareness in general. There were so many other ways of intuiting and becoming aware of lives outside our own. It made sense, in the dark, to believe the dead to be near.

Lying still in bed, Sallie tried to do the relaxation exercises taught her in the clinic by Winfred Levin. First she tautened the muscles in her feet, then let them go floppy.

Calves tightened, then relaxed. Knees tight, then loose. Yet tonight the muscles remained stubbornly taut. The thought that Rosie was in the room, might not merely lean over her but touch her, was a terrible one.

It was strange that not long after having this intolerably frightening thought she had fallen into the deep sleep of childhood. How long she slept she could not tell. In her dream, she was crawling along a forest floor, thick with pine needles. She was being pursued by a predator, unseen from behind trees. She knew he was there because of the smell of his cigarette.

It was the tobacco smell that woke her up. The cigarette was not alight, but she could smell that a smoker was near. The acrid sensation in her sinuses was unmistakable. The smell mingled with others, more animal, rodenty. Male sweat. As she regained consciousness, she listened to the darkness and heard breathing.

She managed to ask, 'Who's there?' but the tremble in her voice actually added to her own terror. She had fallen asleep ready to confront a woman from the spirit world. Now, automatic physical responses came into play. She still wore two pairs of pants – her own panties and Charles's – but she felt so sorry she had removed her jeans. It was going to be so horribly easy for him!

That it should be happening here, in this bed, of all places. She had always feared she would lose her virginity by an act of rape. This was one of the reasons she found the idea of any activity in that area so disgusting and why she was so sure that Charles would be gentle enough to limit himself to just holding, stroking, kissing, but not trying what that New Zealand creep Hugh had suggested to her! She was going to put up a fight. If this bastard in the dark thought he was getting her without a table lamp crashing into his skull, without an electric light bulb broken into his cheeks, he was very much mistaken. And yet such brave and heartbroken angry thoughts were themselves overwhelmed by terror of what he was going to do. She hated so much, so very, very much, the idea of what men had between their legs. Jokes about it, so frequent a part of childhood conversation, had sometimes made her want to throw up.

The breathing continued in the dark and with it the ratty, tobaccoy smell. She opened her mouth, this time to scream. As she did so, the full-throated roar she had wanted to let out came only as a little gasp. The door of the room opened. It stayed open. She could hear footsteps, rapidly moving away down the carpeted, creaking boards. Her visitor had left her.

Most astoundingly, she fell asleep again. When the dawn woke her through the curtainless windows at half past six, and she lay in bed, taking in the familiar shapes of the room, she supposed she had had a bad dream. Then she remembered the unpleasant smells, and by inhaling she thought she could still discern them in the air. He had been real, her night visitor. Rosie, triumphant from her silver frame, gradually became visible in the pale-grey daylight.

Chapter Fifteen

'Now, where the hell's it gone?'

Gloria was in the foulest of moods, and was rattling and rummaging through kitchen drawers with a fury.

Some instinct had made Sallie keep out of her way until the arrival of the Artegalls. Once the children were seated at their breakfast, Sallie had brightly said that she would leave them with Gloria, that she wasn't hungry. Gloria had made as if to speak to her. Sallie could tell that something was 'up'. She felt that Gloria had somehow figured out that she was now sleeping in Charles's room. Sallie intended, if she was brave enough, to tell Gloria that this was none of her business, not any more. But together with this mood of bravado there was a childish fear that Gloria would tell her off, be angry.

While the children ate their breakfast, Sallie had washed her hair, in preparation for Lucy Artegall's arrival. She was giving her au pair a day off, so had brought Simon, the toddler, with her. This, and the presence of Lucy herself in the kitchen, made it mercifully impossible for Gloria to have anything out with Sallie.

'Bloomin' thing. I *keep* losing knives!'

'I keep all mine on a rack,' said Lucy. 'No, Simon, come back.'

The little fellow was stomping towards the edge of the table, his precarious progress suggesting to any adult observer a range of possible calamities – that he would knock his head against the sharp end of the furniture, that he would clutch at the oilskin tablecloth and pull it off, that he would manage to reach some fruit and squidge and squash and mess it up.

To Sallie's eyes he was appalling, repellent. His walk was like that of a very drunken man, strutting about the place, not caring what he wrecked, yet arrogantly suggestive that he owned the place. He had a round, fat face and his lower lips stuck out. His shock of blond hair was lovingly combed. It was evident that Lucy worshipped him. Sallie wondered at the power of maternal love. The logical reaction to this selfish little presence in the room, which was drawing all attention to itself and interrupting any interesting conversation, would have been to kick it.

'But that's my little kitchen devil gone and the big Sabatier. He's a big fellow.'

'Growing all the time,' said Lucy adoringly.

'I mean my carving knife. I don't like to think of one of the children . . . Sallie you haven't . . .'

'Of course not!' exclaimed Sallie, a little too quickly; she felt herself blushing very deeply. She could feel Gloria staring at her hard.

The four older children – Oliver and Freya, Michael and Frances – had gone riding with Rob for a couple of hours. Lucy was having coffee. Sallie would love to have taken her out of the kitchen, so that they could chat without Gloria's lowering presence.

'Ted said one of his hammers went for a walk the other day and all,' said Gloria. 'A hammer – and now knives.'

She spent an inordinate amount of time searching for the knives. It gave Sallie a quiet satisfaction to note her dismay, her irritation. At the same time, Sallie realised she was paying a price for this pleasure: the longer Gloria searched for the knives, the less time Sallie would have with Lucy.

The knives had been necessary. She had taken the small one about a week ago. The larger knife she had removed this morning, while Gloria was in the larder yelling about who wanted baked beans with their sausage. She had quietly slipped back upstairs and concealed the knife in her trusty knapsack, wrapped round inside her rainbow-striped sweater with Ted's hammer. She was not going to spend another night in that house with a man at large in it.

Had her own bedroom been invaded by a rapist, she would naturally have raised an alarm. It was more difficult, because the man had come into the room she shared with Charles. Waking, she had been visited with the by now familiar sensation of wondering whether a terrifying experience had been 'just her imagination'. But she had not invented that tobacco smell and that breathing.

A Quint? A male ghost? Some former household retainer or groundsman, pacing the corridors of the old house at night in search of maiden flesh? This was too sensational. She suspected that the man had been Rob or Ted. In both cases, she had disliked the way they had leered at her when first introduced. No doubt they knew how to deactivate the burglar alarm and enter the house freely.

Ted, the older one, with swept-back oily hair, had specifically asked her whether she was all on her own at night. He had smiled in a way which she now recognised to be highly inappropriate. All his talk of his 'missus' only served to confirm that, in spite of being aged about sixty, he was still ferociously active, his mind swirling with filth. He might come for her, but she would get him with the knife or hammer, his oily head cracked to gore. Even if she did not succeed in killing him, which was what he deserved, she would have no hesitation in punishing the part of the body which intended her such evil. For that, the larger sharp knife was required.

This was the reason that, in spite of the really horrible nature of what had occurred in Charles's bedroom, Sallie could not entirely prevent herself from smiling while Gloria crashed and rummaged and cursed.

Was Gloria somehow *behind* the plot? Was it this truly horrible woman's idea that they could frighten Sallie away from what was rightfully hers – Charles and Staverton? Sallie remembered Gloria's reaction to her screaming fit when she had seen the apparition. She had not come running out to see what was wrong. She said she hadn't heard it, but that was obviously a lie. No, what she had done was to *call up Ted on her mobile*. There was probably a bit too much intimacy between her and Ted? Sallie had noted among her college friends that those who indulged in filthiness were not content to do it simply once or twice. They did it all the time, week after week, day after day. When they were not trying to do it, they were talking about, making jokes about it, filling one another's minds with lascivious and lewd thoughts. They spoke like everyone in the world wanted to do it – not seeming to realise if they ever read a book, that all the great spiritual leaders, from Plato to Jesus to Buddha, taught that celibacy was the only path to wisdom.

It was God's curse on the human race that they could

only be born by this degrading and utterly revolting procedure. But that was it. Once done, there was absolutely no need to go repeating it, again and again like uncontrolled animals. To think of a woman like Gloria, over fifty, speaking of the need to go home to her husband at nights . . . And she said such things in front of the children, who probably also thought it was funny to make jokes about that sort of thing. What was it Michael had said? That Sallie was 'gay at tennis'. Gay? Until she went to Carver, Sallie, while not being drawn to gay activities as such, had felt sympathetic towards gay people, especially women, since she had assumed that they just hugged, rather than doing the other thing. It was Lorrie, as a matter of fact, who with a slightly pained expression had explained what some of their lesbian friends liked to do.

'You're kiddin', aren't you, Sallie? You know what lesbians do?' When she had been told, Sallie felt so weak that she felt she ought to go to the bathroom. How could these people look one another in the face again after doing something like that? How could they – she choked at the question – how could they eat, ever again?

College, both Shaker and Carver, had been a hellish series of obstacles: clubs, socials, dinners, evenings out with pals, in which her various fellow students had been trying to get off with one another and by extension trying to pervert her into that kind of activity. At least England had been a welcome escape and she was now within sight of finding, in kind, tolerant Charles, a man who would look after her, cherish her, enrich her, enfold her, without asking for anything of that nature. How could a coarse person like Gloria be expected to understand a thing like that? So, maybe it had been Gloria who set up the whole thing – arranged for Sallie to be raped the previous evening? If she had not woken up and cried out, might it not be the case that Sallie would already . . . It was too horrible to contemplate.

'Well,' said Gloria at last, 'I give up. I'll have to peel these apples with a blunt old table knife. It's set us all back half an hour.'

'Simon, darling . . . not the banana.'

'Why don't we take him outside . . .' Sallie suggested. The sentence, if she had ruled the world, would have ended 'and smash his head in'. But she said, 'and play with him on the lawn, or have a little look at the goldfish?'

'That's tempting fate – the fishpond.' The ever-indulgent mother laughed. 'But, good idea, let's go and get a breath of fresh air.'

It was while they were on the terrace that Sallie made the cruel realisation that Lucy Artegall was not on her side at all.

She plunged straight in, when alone with Lucy, by asking, 'Have you known Charles long?'

'Lord, don't ask. It's – don't pull the flowers, Simon. We first met over twenty years ago when we were still in our teens. It's fifteen years, I should think, I've been his neighbour. Ever since he inherited this place. I'd known him a bit before he came into it. Simon, no! No – not a flower, darling.'

'And you knew his wife?'

Lucy sighed. 'She's a really good friend – so of course it's been hard.'

Sallie noticed but tried to disregard the use of the present tense in that sentence. 'She was your friend?'

'Still is – when I see her – which makes it very difficult – especially with Charles's very firm – well, what you might call the rules he has set up. I probably shouldn't speak like this to you, Sallie. After all – no offence – but you'll be gone soon. I don't know how it has all struck you. Gloria's wonderful and the children cope pretty well. But it is . . . Well, I love Charles and always will, but I think he's doing the wrong thing. I think it is cruel and – well, stupid.'

'Excuse me?' Sallie felt real indignation that Lucy Artegall, who had seemed such a sensible and friendly person, should be speaking about Charles in this way.

'I don't know how much you were told? I mean one school holidays, the children had a marvellous time. Charles had them to stay in the flat in London. Of course they wanted to see their mother as well. *She is their mother.* Simon, darling, no! Come to Mummie. Come here, Simon. You could say it was silly of Rosie, after all the court orders, and affidavits, and injunctions and de-dah, de-dah, de-dah, but Christ Almighty, all she did was have them over to her flat and take them out – I think she took them to Fortnum's for Christ's sake. But the fuss Charles made! He has liter-ally forbidden Rosie to see the children *ever*. Of course, being a lawyer, he has got away with it, but I think it's – well, I know Rosie did wrong, but it was four years ago now and – well, it's so obviously hard on the children.'

They walked for a while in silence.

A number of the old symptoms crept up on Sallie. She had once described these to a doctor in terms which recalled such 'out of the body' experiences as are felt by patients coming round from anaesthetic. Dreams and hallucino-genic states had also been invoked to describe the feeling: also metaphors of falling through the air, or through water, with no support. She was trying very hard to get a hold of reality and one cog was not engaging with another; the wheels were going round and round in the mud without the car moving.

Lucy was saying things about a dead woman. Lucy was speaking of Rosie as if she were still alive.

The terrible pain caused by these words hit Sallie savagely. There must be some mistake. They could not have the simplicity of truth. Lucy must be wrong. Or Sallie must be mishearing. That was it! She had misheard. Whatever difficulties there had been between Charles and his wife had been *in the past*. And then she had *died*.

'Apart from anything else,' Lucy was saying, 'it is so hard on the children. I don't know how you find them?'

Sallie was making gestures with her head, wiggling it from side to side. She was not exactly shaking it to imply a negative, but this was almost what it looked like.

'Not so good?' pursued Lucy. 'Because, you see, with me they are always controlled. In some ways too controlled. Have they spoken about their mother to you, then? Perhaps it's easier with a comparative stranger.'

'No, no. Not at all.'

'They don't speak of Rosie?'

'Never.'

'This is it, you see. But they must talk about her when they are alone together? That's what I think. In fact – do you know what I think?'

'I'm sorry – you must excuse me . . .' Sallie's words were mumbled, perhaps actually inaudible to Lucy.

'I think they *do* speak to her – on the telephone. I'm sure they've done it from our house – there's a mobile number on our telephone bill. I teased Patrick about it – said it was his secret girlfriend!' She yelped nervously. 'But it's turned up on several dates, and each date that someone has used our phone to ring this number has been a day that Michael and Frances have been over to play with us. So you see – Patrick says I'm wasted, ought to have my own detective agency! They *are* in touch with Rosie.'

'Their mother? They are in touch with . . . ?'

'Don't you think? It wouldn't be natural, would it, for them to keep away from her altogether as Charles insists? Okay, she was a naughty girl – poor Rose!'

It was afterwards, long afterwards, during the evening of solitude in her bedroom that Sallie devoted such hours of speculation to what form Rosie's naughtiness had taken. What could she have done that was so heinous that Charles had forbidden her access to her own children? In that moment in the garden, walking with Lucy, she was still hoping that the words spoken did not correspond to the truth, that there must be some other explanation for what Lucy was saying. Perhaps Lucy had been put up to torturing Sallie – but by whom? Was it all an elaborately malicious joke, an English tease?

'My dear,' Lucy was saying. 'Are you all right? You look as pale as a ghost.'

Chapter Sixteen

Afterwards. Afterwards lasted for ever. You could lie still, you could walk about, you could pace the room, you could try to answer all their goddamned questions, but it was still going to last for ever.

So, in a sense, it no longer mattered what levels of reality, or hyperreality, she was remembering, still less whether the events assembled themselves inside her head in the 'right' order. Right as in Tuesday goes before Wednesday, as in A goes before B, and B before C. Who arranged that in any case? What bastard suddenly decided we had to arrange letters in alphabetical order? What kind of control freak was he? You can be assured it was a male.

She was endlessly being 'evaluated'. They had done these tests on her before, back home, in the clinic after the trouble she had with Kimberley. This place was very different. They were aggressive, obviously trying to make out she was some kind of homicidal maniac who was a danger to the community. She had told them, over and over, that she had not intended to kill a kid. This was not her intention. The so-called evidence presented by Lorrie, who had turned against her, or Mrs Kenner, of all people, whom they had managed to contact, was not evidence at all.

The lawyers – well, lawyers could be expected to side with Charles, who was a lawyer. He was so utterly ruthless to her, so merciless. She had asked repeatedly to see him, to explain what had happened, to tell him that if anyone should be on trial it was his wife, or his neighbour Lucy Artegall. Not her, not Sallie Declan!

They said that he did not want to speak to her and that he was anyway too upset. Of course he was upset, he had lost a kid, that was bound to be upsetting. No one seemed to have appreciated the fact that she too was upset, deeply upset, and hurt and still hurting inside, to believe that Charles would think her capable of murdering one of his beloved children. That was just so very hurtful.

Gloria should have been on trial too. She had set the whole thing up, hadn't she? Not the killing, Sallie granted her that. But what a sneaky thing to do, to get Ted to patrol the house at nights.

There had been some suspicion for a long time. Sallie could not work out for how long they had suspected that Rosie was sleeping in the house. Rob was in on the conspiracy. Gloria had said darkly, 'Well, he would be.' She implied what, exactly, by that? That Rob had been one of Rosie's lovers? Was that it?

Rosie was a whore. She deserved the death sentence that Sallie had meted out to her. If Charles could only be persuaded to meet Sallie she would have been able to explain everything to him, all of it.

He had found out some five years previously that Rosie was persistently unfaithful to him. Rosie was one of those truly disgusting people, whom Sallie had always abominated. In addition to her – habits – with men, Rosie also was heavily into drugs. There had been a groundsman at Bly. Mr Quint – she had done it with Quint, she had done it . . . That wasn't it. No, Rosie had taken lovers and snorted cocaine – at Staverton. The place was called Staverton. Rosie had used drugs. She had used the London flat, not only for drugs but for sleeping with her supplier, a Jamaican boy about ten years her junior. In Charles's bed.

Sallie could no longer remember the order in which all this information had come to her, nor how much of it was true, or made up inside her head, or supplied by Lucy Artegall. The narcotics and sedatives they gave her in the prison, nuthouse, hospital – whatever – made Sallie's head heavy much of the time and it was extremely difficult to put her thoughts in any kind of coherent shape. When she did so, she was aware of thought as a creative act, and she could not always be certain that she was remembering with accuracy, rather than simply being dragged along involuntarily by a sickening and uncontrollable daydream.

Yes, Lucy Artegall – and Lorrie? Yes, Lorrie had e-mailed at some stage that Charles had placed injunctions on his wife, so that she could not come near either him or Staverton or the children. Because of something she had done four or five years ago. It was Lucy, of course it was Lucy, who had supplied the detail of the Jamaican drug dealer. Charles had argued before a judge that his children could easily have come into the room and met this man with their mother. The police had confirmed, when Rosie had been arrested for possession, that she had been taking cocaine and that she had bought it from this male. She admitted the adultery, not only with the Jamaican but with several other men.

How could she have done that when she was married to Charles? He still loved her.

'That's what I find really *maddening* about Charles, you know, Sallie. He still loves Rosie. I think with one part of his stubborn, legalistic brain, he still desperately wants her back. I'll tell you a secret Gloria told me. He still keeps her photograph in his bedroom – after all they've been through, those two, the court battles, the rows – she's still there for him!'

That had been Lucy Artegall during the second of their conversations – Before. There was an absolute gulf fixed between Before and Afterwards. Before was before, when people spoke to Sallie in those normal sorts of ways. After – she was a handcuff case, a nut, someone trundled in the back of vans, attached to other human bodies. That was just the worst, the proximity. In that van, having to be handcuffed to a policewoman, their wrists touching, the sweat of one body pouring towards another body.

Sallie, you're nuts.

That was Before. Lorrie had e-mailed that to her Before. Said she was nuts. Said she had – what was it –

I have now spoken to your Mr Charles Masters again and, Sal, I'm sorry to say this, but I've told him the truth. Sallie, I told you to go back to London. He sounded really nice, said that he was in a real mess since his wife had gone off – he didn't go into details, but it was obviously fairly shattering for him and he did not like doing it, but he had to prevent her from seeing the children until she consented to go for rehab. I did not tell him that you were under the impression that you had seen his wife's ghost. Honestly, Sallie, you're nuts.

'Frances, do you mind me asking you something?'

'What?'

'Your mom – your mom and your dad – they . . . Your mom isn't dead, is she?'

'Course not – whatever made you think that?'

Frances had gone extremely red when questioned about it. Naturally, once the truth had dawned, Sallie knew it was her duty to hunt Rosie down. Sallie had seen her, once by the sheds and another time in the summer house. There was every reason to suppose that she was in fact staying at Staverton, perhaps with the connivance of Rob. So Sallie would hunt her down. Rosie had been seeing the kids.

What was her job, for God's sake? Why had Charles hired her? He had done so so that she should look after his children every hour of the day – and, as she now realised, for every hour of the night as well. Of course the children did not need to be guarded by Sallie because they were in danger of physical attack by Gloria or Ted or Rob, or a passing rambler. They did not need to be protected from the Artegalls. Charles had hired Sallie to prevent the kids from seeing their mother. He had obviously done so because he had the same views as Sallie about filthiness.

If he had not shared these views, he'd have been laid back. Okay, go ahead, do whatever it is you want to do with these men, take your filthy narcotics, why not ask the kids to join in too while you are about it . . . That's what he could have done. Instead, no. He'd been a responsible adult, he'd done all the things which would make people think he was a hard man, and that had taken real courage when almost no one except Sallie, perhaps absolutely no one, had ever seen through to the real Charles, the soft-hearted Charles who was hurting so badly inside. He had been brave enough to want his wife kept absolutely out of his kids' lives. He had

used the full force of the law to get Sallie to be the one
who looked after them. Sallie, and not Rosie. And why?
Because from the very first moment he had met Sallie, he
was talking about taking her to the opera, and showing her
England, and her being like the kids' true mom. That was
the truth of the matter, the rest was just bullshit.

Naturally, she had to find where that whore, that bad
woman, was hiding and stop her filling the minds of innocent children with thoughts that would poison them for
the rest of their lives. If Sallie had not done this, she
would have been failing, utterly, in her commitments to
Charles. What sort of a basis was that for her whole future
relationship with Charles and his children?

They were all speaking like she was some kind of, of, of
– nanny for Jesus's sake. That was what she was called in
the newspaper article she had read. It was a few days old.
It had been lying around in the room where they took her
clothes off. The humiliation of that stripping. Had they
any idea how much that had hurt her, the way they had
made her undress those women, those women in uniform?
That had been Afterwards. They had told her to undress
and to put her clothes in a bag, which would be taken
away. And she had been left standing there, completely
naked. She had asked if they had really wanted her to
remove all her clothes and the larger of the two uniformed
women, a great black giantess, had said yes, everything.
She had said it so cruelly. The wrench had been parting
from Charles's socks. They were too big for Sallie's feet,
naturally, but she had taken to wearing them tucked into
the elastic of her panties. How could the prison wardresses
know what these garments had meant to Sallie, when they
asked her to put them in the plastic bag. Or 'the plastic
bag provided' as they said.

Provided what? Who provided? Sallie, for a moment, had enjoyed some intellectual superiority to these uniformed bitches – not out loud, of course. But she had played a little with the ambiguity of the phrasing. Put the clothes in the bag, provided you want to; put them in the bag, provided you can distinguish between the bag and the clothes.

'You don't need a bra, do you?'

That had been the black woman's remark. She'd just stared and stared at Sallie when she made this comment, like Sallie was some specimen on a tray being carried into a laboratory. Her large, clothed arms were folded against an enormous, bulbous front, as she surveyed Sallie's boy chest.

And there had been a small tabloid newspaper sitting beside this woman, with the big headline STATELY HOME KILLER NANNY ARRESTED.

That was her. A stately home killer nanny.

If this ridiculous business was not cleared up she was going to stand trial. And that was what she would be as, day following day, they drove her to court in a van. She would be the nanny who killed the little kid.

They did not keep her well informed about what was going on. She did not know yet whether she was standing trial, or whether they were still evaluating her. The lawyer had been to see her and set out the various options while she was in hospital. She was there for her own protection from other prisoners, who had a particularly vindictive view of those who killed children. She was also being evaluated by psychiatrists to see whether it would be appropriate to plead diminished responsibility. There was even a question of whether she would be psychologically strong enough to endure a trial. That was what the lawyer had said. It was a female lawyer, which Sallie found singularly annoying somehow. She had half hoped that there would be a possibility of getting Charles to defend her. It was one of the things she had hoped to discuss with him, if he would only get in touch with her.

'Sallie, we have to work with the materials we have, and from the position we are in. We have to be realistic. As I see things, the facts are not in dispute. The question is not whether you . . . whether you killed . . . The question is not whether you did it, but whether we plead guilty to murder or whether we enter a plea of guilty to manslaughter, with diminished responsibility; or whether we go down the option of absolute non-responsibility and request your hospitalisation here to be put on a semi-permanent basis. Frankly, a lot is going to depend on whatever evidence the police bring forward, and on how we get on with the Crown Prosecution Service. You understand that? Are you familiar with the process in this country? The Crown Prosecution Service . . .'

She was not familiar with the legal niceties and she was only listening with part of her ear. It just seemed so grotesque that this lawyer, supposedly on her side, was unable to see that the correct plea was that it was an accident.

She had not meant to kill a child, she had meant to kill Rosie. And Rosie had thoroughly deserved to die.

'She is the children's mother' – Lucy Artegall. That day. The day everything altered. 'It's not so very unreasonable that they should want to see their own mother.'

Rounding the corner of the terrace, looking down to the summer house, she had seen them. Playing cards with Rosie in the summer house. Now she understood the murmurings at night that regularly came from the little girl's bedroom. Now she understood why both the children were so happy to let Sallie say goodnight to them early each night and go to her own room to work on Henry James. They never pleaded, like kids were meant to, can we stay up half an hour longer. They just trotted off to the girl's bedroom happy as anything.

They were concealing their mother in one of their bedrooms. The woman was sleeping in the house. The woman who had done . . . those things, those truly disgusting things with her body, and with so very many men, was prepared to put her soiled limbs, her impure whore's body into the sheets of little children.

Everything was all right until Gloria found out.

It seemed that after the incident of Sallie's scream – the first time she had seen Rosie by the stables – Gloria and Ted had formed a plan. No one told Sallie this. She had merely inferred it, in the long hours of Afterwards in her white, locked room, staring at the ceiling, staring at the tiled walls, staring at the barred window, high in the white walls, and staring at the white sky. Gloria had heard her scream, Ted had heard it, and they both knew what had caused it. Perhaps they did not realise that she believed Rosie to be a visitant from beyond the grave; but they knew that Sallie had seen something disturbing and it probably did not take long to work out what had happened. At some stage the children had arranged to meet up with their mother and allow her back to Staverton. Rob was in on the conspiracy, even allowing Rosie to ride Peperoni with the children in their canters up past Farrer's Copse.

This was not Sallie's fantasy. It belonged to Before. She had heard the fight between Gloria and Rob, or some of it.

'If kids want to see their mother . . .'

'It's the law, Rob, surely you can see that. Charles has been quite clear about that from day one. The law has forbidden Rosie to see those kids and . . .'

'The law – don't give me that. Would you not see your kids just because some old tosser in a wig told you . . .'

'Rob that isn't the point. My job's on the line, Rob Bennett, and if you . . .'

'Oh, so now we understand. It's not about mums and kids, it's about jobs.'

'Rob, you know as well as I do that Charles . . .'

That was what she had heard in the stable, while she paced, that last day, looking for Rosie's hiding place at Staverton. The shrubbery, the sheds, the summer house. She had examined them all for traces of her prey.

Ted had known for some days. He had been nosing around the house at night, looking for Rosie. He'd been coming in the bedrooms and thought, when he came into Charles's room and breathed over Sallie, that he had found Rosie. It was Rosie who came into that room in the morning, of course, and made the bed. It was Rosie's perfume that filled the house. It was Rosie who had told the police that Sallie slept in Charles's bed.

Over and over and over they asked her about that, as if it were of the slightest relevance and as if it were anyone's business but hers and Charles's alone. This was something between them. The police, and the doctors, had naturally wanted to make the line of questioning as filthily suggestive as possible. Had she, ever; would she, was it her intention, that sort of dirt. She responded, when they began getting off on her love life with Charles, with an absolute and dignified silence. She would not speak of these things to the doctors. They had examined her. They knew she was a virgin. For what had felt like days, they had prodded her, touched her, looked at her. They had shone lights in her eyes, looked down her throat, peered into her ears, sounded her chest. There was no part of her person which they did not try to violate. And they had then taken further possession of her by means of narcotics, forcing her to take bigger and bigger doses so that time stood still, and the borderlands between appearance and reality were really impossible to distinguish.

'Obviously, Sallie' – that female lawyer again – 'character witnesses are going to be important, whatever avenue we explore. You say that Professor Helstone would be willing to . . .'

He had written to her, her old Hell's Angel. He had written a letter which they had allowed her to read, but it was then confiscated. It was a really sweet letter. It had made her cry. He had said he hoped she was getting all the help she required, both medical and legal, and wondered whether, while she was confined in the hospital, she would like to continue with her thesis work.

They had allowed Helly to come and see her. She had not wanted this. At first, she had been pleased by the idea of a visitor, any visitor, who might take her mind off the truly terrible situation. Did they have a death penalty in England? She had really no idea.

He had been tongue-tied, sitting there in the room, opposite a table, with the wardress sitting on an upright chair in one corner, listening to what he had to say.

'Obviously, mm, mmm, now could be a time for some more general reading around the subject – perhaps you haven't had as much time as, mm, mmm, as it were.'

He had brought a plastic shopping bag full of books, which they had allowed him to leave behind for her. J. I. M. Stewart's *Eight Modern Writers* and *Nostromo*, which she had never read, and some Kipling short stories, and a book called *Henry James and the Ghostly*. He had also brought a book about the Benson family.

Sallie could not read any more. She was unable to concentrate upon words on the page. If she had been able to speak, she would have said this to Professor Helstone, as he sat there, twiddling his thumbs and looking, pitifully, at her, as he yammered about Henry James and the late-Victorian, early-twentieth-century literary scene. Not a syllable came to her lips. It was not possible to talk. She had tried to write to him. Was it during the few hours after his visit, or was it several days, or even several weeks, later?

Because the psychiatrists and the lawyer and the police had made her utter sentences she no longer believed to be true, it was strangely impossible to speak when Helstone came, even though she was overwhelmed by his obvious desire to be kind. The same had been true when her mom was led into the room.

It was surreal to see her own mother in this white room, like a figure stepping into a dream. Mom had been her predictable, embarrassing self. Had this been before or after Hell's Bells came? It was already a long time ago, or felt like it. Mom had been a stream of incoherent and illogical questions. At first she had been all lovey-dovey to her little Sallie pet. Mom had put on a lot of weight since Christmas, she really filled that scarlet pants suit. She had cut her hair rather mercilessly short and dyed it a lighter shade of blonde. By her lights, she had smartened up – more than could be said for Sallie, who slumped, in her jeans and sweatshirt, feeling and looking a wreck. The wardress stopped Mom trying to hug her and that had been a relief, and then, when Sallie had slumped in her chair again, a discarded rag doll, and Mom had sat down opposite, the questions had begun. Hadn't she said it was a mistake to take a job looking after kids, after all the trouble she'd had with Mrs Kenner? Did she know Mrs Kenner had sold her story to the *New York Post*? It had been syndicated round the world. Eighty thousand dollars Mrs Kenner had made out of it so far, with photographers coming round to take pictures of her bathroom and buy up the pictures of Jakie when he was just a little kid. Of course, Jakie was eleven now – they were not playing down the glue-sniffing incident, which had happened at school about three years after Sallie had seen the last of him.

The scars left by the killer nanny were not just physical, that kind of stuff. Mrs Kenner plugging it for all it was worth. For much *more* than it was worth. Eighty thousand dollars, can you just *imagine*? All this blabbed out to Sallie in front of the wardress with no thought for what kind of trouble it was going to get her into.

After about half an hour of it and Sallie not answering, not saying one single word, Mom had begun to get mad. She'd started to say how she'd flown three thousand miles on money she couldn't afford to see her daughter and she thought it was no more than common decent courtesy to speak to your own mother when she'd come all that way. Said some stuff about her nerves being all to pieces and how she was going to have to move house, couldn't stay in Muncie, that was for sure. Not with reporters sniffing around and saying killer nanny's mom stands by her little daughter. And frankly, why did Sallie think she would stand by her if this was all the welcome she was going to get? Mom had started to shout really loud, stuff about Sallie being like her dad, and all evil and rotten, and the Gestapo hags had then stood up and shown her out of the room. Mom had come again after that. Was it the next day? You couldn't work out time in this place. It was a much shorter visit, very subdued, and Sallie seemed to remember that a doctor came with her that time. Someone in a white coat anyway. Mom was crying and saying she was going home to Muncie now, but she'd be back to see her little girl and she knew her own little Sallie wouldn't hurt a fly.

Goddamn it, Mom, I've killed a kid. I am not indicted for killing a fly. I killed a kid.

Of course, she had said nothing. The person in a white coat had allowed her mother to hold her. Sallie had not been starving, but she knew that her weight had gone right down since she came to this place. Mom had said she was like a little bird.

'Are they feeding you in this place?'

It was like school, the way she heard Mom still asking about that as they led her away. Did they make sure Sallie ate? How about if she had a word with the kitchen staff and asked them if maybe they could cook some of Sal's favourite dishes?

She'd gone. The relief was terrible. Sallie had cried for weeks, perhaps for years, it felt like for ever she'd cried when her mom had gone. She so wanted a rerun of both visits, she wanted to reach out to Mom, and stop her jabbering nonsense, and just talk to her quietly, naturally; ask about neighbours in Muncie and Nancy Lloyd, Mom's special friend who worked as a secretary at the dentist – Mr Delgado – and whether Mr Delgado still had those dachshunds, and some stuff at church, and whether the minister, Reverend McCudden, had been cleared yet of that supposed irregularity with the choir funds. She loved Mom's small town gossip, and this was what she wanted now, more than anything, to hear. But the chance to hear it was gone and with it had gone all her innocent, lost American childhood. While her mother had actually been with her, the presence of the woman had been too much. First she had felt embarrassed, horribly embarrassed – both because of the way Mom spoke and behaved, but also because of what had happened. It just was so awful to see in her mother's desolated face just what she had done to this woman by getting involved in this horrible accident.

Then, when Mom had started on about Jakie Kenner and Mrs Kenner making money out of the newspapers, Sallie had been revisited by all the old feelings of rage with her. This was meant to be her mother sitting here, and it sounded like she completely endorsed the police view and the tabloid journalists' view that Sallie was indeed a murderer.

You are not a murderer if you kill someone by mistake – when you had in fact been trying to kill another person altogether – when you had been trying to kill someone who thoroughly deserved to die. The aeroplanes who dropped bombs on Berlin, trying to kill Adolf Hitler, are not usually classified as murderers because they happened to kill innocent bystanders, some of them no doubt kids.

Unfortunately, Sallie could not say these words to her mother. She could not say any words. She could see the rage and hurt on her mother's face the longer the silence went on. And when – it was during the second visit, no? – her mom had asked the doctor about it, and he'd said it was normal, nothing to worry about – Sallie was a kid again, a kindergarten pupil, while Mom and teacher talked about her over her head.

They were lumbering about the house looking for Rosie – Gloria, Ted – and not really understanding what they were doing. They were just obeying Charles's orders, but they did not see why it was so vital that Rosie should be gotten rid of – because she was corrupting those kids, and if she was still there when Charles got back from Hong Kong, Sallie was the one who was to blame.

She had to vindicate herself by getting rid of Charles's wife. The humiliation of discovering her mistake had been terrible. The mistake, that is, of supposing Rosie to be a ghost. Lucy Artegall could not know what confusion and pain she had caused by her revelation that morning in the garden. She only had half a mind on it, anyway, since the bombshell had no sooner been dropped than she was chasing after Simon down the gravel path and lifting him as, grazed and caterwauling, he had sprawled drunkenly face down on the ground.

Rosie was alive! And Sallie had become so used to thinking she was dead – knowing she was dead – treating her like she was dead. It was something she had grown not merely used to, but happy with, very happy, and she intended, when her anger had simmered down to manageable proportions, to return matters to the status quo as soon, and as unambiguously, as possible.

Of course, it was a wrestle in her head. Part of her brain was saying, 'Lorrie is right, get out of this *now*, just go, get out and go back to London.' And the other could not tear herself away, could not spoil the chance of happiness with Charles, could not allow one drug-crazed, corrupt, flame-headed hooker to come back and spoil everything – not only for her but for Charles too. During the afternoon of that day her discovery had thrown her into a hypersensitive condition. She was overexcited, unable to eat or swallow, almost at times unable to breathe.

Rosie was meant to be dead. One of the important texts of critical theory for her – Todorov? Stanley E. Fish? They were a little muddled right now in her head – said how reading is a creative act, thinking is a creative act. Maybe it was Barthes. We make our own text. Each reader of a text brings to birth for herself a new book and each thinking person brings to pass a new truth. There's no such thing as a concrete reality, with us going around like so many recording machines or cameras taking impressions of it. We make reality. For her, the reality had been, ever since she came to Bly, that Rosie was dead.

Rosie actually *was* Miss Jessel? Maybe that was going too far, but not so very far. Think of the drugs, the inappropriate behaviour, the B.L. (Oh, as a late teenager she'd devised this euphemism inside her head, to prevent herself even having to say words which made you think of males doing those things? . . . So, she'd made it Between Legs – that was what she called it, B.L. for short. It was her own private code, not an expression she used with her friends. B.L. Alert, B.L.!! If someone got raunchy in their talk. And then she'd come to London? And the other grads in the hostel in Mabledon Place had started, like, saying they would be going that day to the British Library, or would maybe see her in the British Library? And it was all, 'See you at the BL! Are you going to the BL today?' No wonder that place had given her a nervous breakdown.)

But Rosie and the Jamaican pusher, Rosie and Rob in all likelihood – B.L., B.L., narcotics and B.L. With the kids about, maybe in the next room. Could anything more thoroughly appalling be imagined – teaching kids that that kind of behaviour was appropriate, was decent, was normal? A knife or a hammer would simply – it would be the matter of a moment, when that moment came – put things into shape, restore the status quo. Rosie had been 'dead' to Sallie from the moment of the interview with Charles.

Gloria wasn't going to admit to Charles that Rosie was at large in the house. He had paid her, and Ted, and Rob, to keep the slut away from the children. If they failed in this one simple task, what justification, frankly, was there for their existence at Bly? Of course they were going to cover up their mistakes to Charles. Of course – hindsight made this as clear as day – they were going to blame Sallie for everything that had happened.

That Victorian painting – *The Scapegoat*! Sallie had wept so much when she saw it reproduced in a book. She guessed it was somewhere in London? It was a pity, such a pity that she had not taken more time in her first months in the City to see the galleries. Now there would be no chance to see paintings, sculptures, concerts. Those promised opera nights with Charles, she and him, sitting in the grandest box in the Opera House, while the crowds all asked themselves who's that with Charles Masters? Who? That beautiful lady in the bunches, the one in the fleece top with teddy bears on it? Shouldn't she be in a ballgown, for God's sake, a tiara? No, you see, because frankly, Charles Masters is not quite so *bourgeois*: he does not need to dress women up like Barbie dolls to show them he loves them – this is his soulmate, his love. It is Sallie Declan and she's just sitting there, not because she has fancy clothes, not because she . . .

But it wasn't going to happen now. That was Before and this was Afterwards. All through a stupid, dumb mistake, or all through someone else's malice. Gloria had taken all her hate, all her guilt at what had happened, and heaped it on to *The Scapegoat*. It stood there, shivering on its thin legs, with the Dead Sea in the background. The Children of God had driven it out into the wilderness. She recalled a sermon by Reverend McCudden about it, how the

Children of God couldn't carry their hurts and their griefs and their inadequacies, so they heaped them all on this animal. And all the bad feelings inside them, and all the things that made them feel real dirty and like they needed a bath, only they just couldn't wash themselves clean, all those real bad things they heaped on the goat. And they drove it far into the Wilderness of Judea, out into the arid desert, where nothing grew, where there was blazing heat by day and freezing cold by night, and there it died. It had carried their sins, just a little goat. That was what Sallie was in this particular case and there could be no doubt about that. A little killer nanny-goat who'd borne their griefs and carried their afflictions. They were all busy trying to say she'd done something wrong, because they all knew they were guilty as hell: Gloria, Ted, Rosie, Mrs Artegall.

People were trying to blame Charles too, saying he had no business dictating the way his children were brought up; saying if he had such strong views about it, maybe he should have stayed home and looked after them instead of going off to Hong Kong. That is very easy to say if, like those who were no doubt saying it, you knew absolutely nothing about the grown-up world of international law, high finance . . . And another thing, if you did not know how he couldn't go to Bly, he'd been too hurt, too goddamned hurt to see much of those kids she was poisoning and filling with dirt.

So there they all were at the tea table yet again, sitting looking at the pale-blue oilcloth with ships sailing all over it, and just about to have their tea – Gloria was standing beside the Aga, and Lucy was there, with Simon, using cottage pie like it was napalm, putting it into his spoon and seeing how many people he could zap with it, and Michael had his head down, slurping in the pie, his favourite, like he hadn't eaten for weeks, and Flora was making her usual attempts at polite conversation. 'Cottage is beef,' she was saying, 'and shepherd's is lamb, really. I can see why shepherd's pie is the name for lamb, 'cause shepherds look after lambs. But why isn't it cowman's pie for beef mince?'

Lucy was one of those grown-ups, even when she wasn't trying to restrain Simon, who did not answer children. She laughed at them. 'Well, I must say that's an original one,' she said.

'Desperate Dan has Cow Pie,' said Oliver Artegall, imitating this evidently Herculean figure, of whom Sallie had never heard, by exaggerated arm and face movements.

Freya, slow on the uptake, said that shepherds lived in cottages too, or they could do.

'Wherever they live, it's a jolly good pie by the look of it,' said Lucy.

'Mum,' protested Oliver, 'how could you tell whether the pie was any good just by looking?'

'It's going down well, anyway,' said Gloria, preening herself with self-satisfaction, 'never fails with kids, cottage pie.'

This remark was so annoying that Sallie shoved her helping of pie to the side of the plate. She wanted to dispute the assertion that Gloria's food was so irresistible that no one could fail to appreciate it. But at that moment the phone rang again – it had been ringing all afternoon, with some frenzy, and Gloria, shooting Sallie a glance of anxiety, answered it.

'Right,' she said firmly. 'All right. Yup. Okay. Well, shall I get her to come to the phone – only we've got a room full of people here, Charles, and . . .'

All day, since realising that Rosie was still alive, Sallie

had been in this hypertense state, this condition where reality was fading in and out of fantasy, where she could not breathe or swallow or eat with ease. And the comings and goings in the house, and the endless ringing of the telephone, and Gloria's muttering into her mobile were, as far as she had been concerned, 'noises off'. Now she was stunned into realising that Charles was talking to Gloria, right now, on the telephone, in this kitchen.

'I'll tell her to take it in the library. Give it ten minutes. Yeah,' Gloria was saying. 'Oh, look, if we don't – what time is it there now? Midnight? Well, look if we don't manage to speak again, I'll expect her midday tomorrow? She's phoning? Norland are ringing to say when she's coming?'

The words flew about, startled birds rising from the trees, settling on no branch of meaning. Norland was a nanny agency. They were expecting a Norland nanny the next day. They were expecting someone to replace Sallie at midday on the morrow. That was what memory told her in the long Afterwards when she went over that day over and over and over. At the time, into her quickened excited consciousness, there came the knowledge that he was there. He was ringing up and asking for her.

'Sallie, my love, that was Charles on the line. Now, he's going to ring up again in about ten minutes, and he thinks maybe if you sat in the library and answered the telephone in there – you know where it is, the phone?'

There had been carefulness in the way Gloria spoke. It was the way you would speak to a dog when you were trying to get it to drop a bone from its jaws. She called Sallie 'my love', but that was just the way she'd've spoken to a kid, trying to calm it down. Gloria did not love Sallie. Gloria had hated her guts from the moment she arrived at Bly and there was one very simple reason for that.

The reason became clear as sunlight to Sallie as she rose triumphantly, leaving her inedible mush on the side of her plate. Charles wanted to speak to her on the telephone. It was one of those moments when you knew exactly what was going to happen before it happened. Charles was calling up because he could not wait until he got back to England to say what he had to say. He was calling to ask Sallie to marry him. That was why Gloria was looking at her strangely, furtively, not quite able to meet her eye.

'If you'll excuse me,' Sallie said exultantly.

Lucy had looked at her so strangely. Sallie shot a nervous glance at the children. How were they going to take the news that, in ten minutes' time, she was going to be their mom? That was a bridge they would cross when they came to it.

She switched on the lights in the library. So much had happened since, sitting on the steps in that room, she had heard Charles's voice on the answering machine, unintentionally recording his conversation with Gloria.

It's the American reference which worries me.

He'd said that, but he couldn't have meant it. If he had been seriously worried then about Lorrie's area code being different from Mrs Kenner's, he was certainly not going to let a little thing like that worry them now. It was hardly going to stand between them and their entire future happiness.

Sallie remembered the patronising way that Gloria had spoken about her that day and the way she had also patronised the Americans in general.

Not at all your brash American type . . . Frannie's being great . . .

If Gloria only knew that she had been overheard by

Sallie, by her future employer, speaking in this glib way, this stupid, insulting way!

Sallie lit a lamp and sat at the large, leather-covered library table, staring at the telephone. She knew that her destiny was about to change, to be determined by the ringing of one little plastic machine. Its noise rang through her like gunshot and her small hand shook as she lifted it. 'Hello?'

'Is that Sallie Declan?'

The use of her surname was disconcerting. It made her stomach heave at once, as did his tone, which was cold, angry and much, much further away than Hong Kong. That voice was from the moon, the lightless, icy moon. 'Charles?'

'Look, Sallie, I'll be brief. I've been in court all day and I've spent the best part of my evening trying to organise things at Staverton. I am asking you to leave there tomorrow morning after breakfast. I don't suppose you need me to tell you why?'

'Charles, listen . . . Charles . . . what is this? What has Gloria been saying about me?'

'Okay, I'll spell it all out. When I interviewed you, I asked you to supply me with two references. You gave the name of Professor Helstone, who has been supervising your thesis but is not in a position to judge your competence as a nanny; and you gave me the name of a Mrs Kenner, of Muncie, Indiana. Only you did not give me Mrs Kenner's true telephone number, did you?'

She had mumbled, almost squeaked, her non-response.

'Are you still following me? Do you need me to go on? You gave me the number of a Miss Loretta Piccioni, didn't you? She has been your college friend at Carver, Ohio, and you thought that she would be prepared to lie for you to cover up an incident that happened when you were looking after Mrs Kenner's son four years ago. Are you still there? Sallie? Are you still there?'

'Yup. I didn't think . . . Look, Charles, none of this matters any more? Right? Look, I am sorry, it was stupid, but . . .'

'Just let me read to you what the intern's report at St Joseph's Hospital, Muncie, Indiana, says about Jakie Kenner on the evening of 27 July 1999. And I would remind you that the patient being described is a child aged six. "Severe contusions not on one side, but on both sides of the head . . . Considerable loss of blood . . . Wounds not compatible with the patient merely having fallen against the faucet, since wounds are to be found on both sides of the skull . . . Only possible conclusion that a blow had been delivered to the side of the head." I now refer you to a slightly later document, which we have managed to procure from the police department at Surbiton, Ohio, which as you know is the police precinct in whose catchment area Carver College is situated. This refers to the wounds inflicted on a Miss Kimberley Markevich . . . Sallie, do I really have to go on? You then were detained at the Bethany Clinic, which is on campus at Carver, for six months as an in-patient and for a further six months as an out-patient with Dr Winifred Levin.'

'Winfred – not Winifred – it's a man's name, Winfred . . . Charles, can you just let me explain . . . If you could only let me explain why I didn't tell you all this when we first met. Look, the kids and me, we've been fine, we've gotten along just great.'

'That is a matter of opinion.'

There was a very long silence.

'Charles, what has Gloria been saying about me?'

'This is no longer really relevant. I only received the fax from the police department in Ohio this afternoon. I should have acted as soon as I had had the whole matter out with Miss Piccioni on the telephone. She admitted, of course, that you had asked her to lie for her, to impersonate Mrs Kenner, which is how the whole matter arose. I blame myself as much as anyone and I certainly do not need or want to go over old history with you. But I am asking you to leave Staverton in the morning.'

An eternity of silence followed before she replied, 'I can't do that, Charles.'

'We have done what we should have done in the first place and engaged an emergency nanny from an agency. Of course, you will be paid, I have asked Gloria to see to all that and I gather she has organised transport – it's a Lymingbourne taxi firm called Chris Cars. They are coming for you at eleven fifteen tomorrow morning. By rights, I should ask you to leave the house at once, but I realise that you will need to pack and make arrangements.'

'Charles, please . . . just listen to me, things have gone much, much too far for this . . .'

In the long Afterwards she had asked herself why she had not blurted out – 'Charles, Rosemary, your wife Rosie, with all her filth and her drugs and her perversions, is sleeping in this house, is sleeping in one of the children's beds! Please believe me, Charles, this is God's own truth and it has been happening right under Gloria's nose, Charles.' If only she had said this, but she didn't. She had feared his anger so much. It was so horribly cold. All that tenderness, when he had been, verbally, making love to her in his London office, wanting them to have long smoochy evenings of opera, and being so sure she was the right mom for his kids – all that warmth and love had vanished from his voice. He had been corrupted, poisoned against her. He had been bewitched.

'I don't think that much more is to be gained by talking, Sallie, quite frankly. I am sorry, it is extremely late here in Hong Kong, way past midnight, and I am just asking you to leave tomorrow morning. If you want me to ring back Gloria and tell her that you must leave at once . . .'

'Of course not.'

'So I have your assurance that you will leave in the morning?'

After another eternal silence, 'In the morning? Is that understood?'

'Good night, Charles.'

She could not go back to the kitchen. They would all know and be whooping with mockery of her. Gloria would have told them while she was out of the room what was happening, how some starched person in uniform was coming down from London in the morning to look after the kids. There would be completely exaggerated and absurd accounts from Gloria about the accident in the bath with Jakie and the Kimberley thing. From the way Gloria was speaking to them, probably, it was like they had the Boston Strangler in the house!

There was, of course, no question of her leaving Staverton tomorrow, or ever. She would have to stay and explain the whole situation to Charles when he returned from Hong Kong. She had never even heard before that an intern at St Joseph's Hospital *had* made a report on the state of Jakie's thick skull. He'd fallen against the faucet for Christ's sake. Maybe to stop the crying, to stop that God-awful noise he was making, she had held his mouth, she honestly could not remember, it was four years ago, maybe a little force had been necessary. Had these people never tried to give a kid a bath?

Of course she had to stay and explain everything to Charles, but there was no need for her any more to do nannying work. The kids could see themselves to bed.

Later – she was not really aware of time any more, because, in effect, she entered Afterwards when Charles Masters hung up on her – Gloria had come knocking on her bedroom door. 'I just wondered if you needed a cup of tea or anything?'

Anyone watching might have been deceived into thinking that Gloria was being kind. Such an innocent stranger, seeing Gloria's concerned expression and hearing the gentle tone – like she was talking to some kind of hospital patient – would have thought the blonde, coarse hag was trying to put Sallie at her ease. She wasn't, she was doing what she'd done from the very beginning, under-mining her. Placing herself in the oh-so-high-and-mighty position; she, Gloria, was the confident one and Sallie was the little jerk who needed cooing at, like she was a nut. Gloria was the one who was staying and Sallie was being thrown out. Well, if she thought that, she was wrong.

'Ken and I are going to spend the night in one of the spare rooms – they have enough of them!' She smiled, triumphant.

What was Ken in hell's name doing in the house? Why couldn't Gloria do without B.L. activity just for eight hours? Could anything be more disgusting? Was this nation obsessed by B.L.? Maybe it was and maybe that explained how it had gone down the pan.

'Excuse me?'

'You'll be all right,' cooed Gloria. 'I can make you a cup of tea. I'll give you a call, shall I, when I've put on the burglar alarm? Only Ken's down in the kitchen and wants to see *Crimewatch.*'

So, while they were downstairs. She had to find Rosie while Gloria and Ken were downstairs. The children were in their rooms? Lucy Artegall had long since gone? She looked at her travelling alarm clock and it said ten past ten. The evening hours, between the telephone call and now, had slipped past in a welter of shock and misery.

She had her flashlight. If she could only find Rosie, confront her, tell her to go, just in God's name *go*! Then the whole nightmare could be resolved. They could see then that she had saved the entire situation. Gloria would be grateful to her because she had saved her job. Wasn't her job to stop Rosie seeing the children? And she had failed. If Sallie got Rosie out of the house before morning, Gloria would be pleased, Ken would be pleased . . . Charles would understand, when he came back, that he actually depended on Sallie. Okay, so an agency nanny would turn up in the morning. That suited Sallie just fine. The kids needed a nanny and, as Lorrie had been right to point out, this was hardly work suitable for Sallie. They needed a nanny and they needed a mom. Sallie was their mom.

You could smell Ken in the house – cigarette smoke permeated the corridors – and somehow you could smell Rosie. She was sure that she could discern that expensive scent. Where was she? In their room – Sallie's and Charles's? That was where she tried first. To Sallie's astonishment, she found that it had been locked. What did that signify? That Ken and Gloria knew of her habit of going in there? That it had been Ken who came in and found her in bed there? Ken who nearly raped her?

She rattled the doorknob furiously. What right had these

people, her servants, to lock her out of her own room in
her own house?

She opened the neighbouring door and saw an open suit-
case, evidently Gloria's and Ken's, with nightclothes and
sponge bags. What did they think they were doing – spying
on her? Spying on her when the dangerous one, the hooker,
was somewhere at large in this house? What kind of crazy
response was that?

Back on her own corridor, she opened Miles's door and
found him there, lying asleep. His lamp was still lit. His
pocket computer chess set was lying on the sheets, his
fingers were almost touching it. So vulnerable, he lay there,
and his eyes were shut. His lips, so rosy red, so delicate,
were curled in that sardonic smile. Was his whore-mom in
the room? And where was Flora?

The thing came to her in an instant as she rampaged to
the girl's room and flung open the door.

'What do you think you are doing?'

Those are the words that were spoken. Spoken to her.
Rosie said them. She was lying there in the child's bed.
Why would they not believe her, however often she told
them that? Rosie, who had utterly degraded herself and
made herself into filth and scum, was lying in a little girl's
bed. She was wearing nightclothes, some kind of nightdress, Sallie was quite able to describe it. They said of course
she could describe it, Rosie was wearing it ten minutes later
when she raised the alarm. She was lying there in the girl's
bed. Flora was nowhere to be seen, Frannie. She just wasn't
there. Sallie was not obliged to say where she had been –
in the bed in Michael's room, the second bed there? Hiding
in a closet? Maybe she'd just gone to the bathroom. The
thing they could not believe was that Frannie was not in
the bedroom, or anyway not visible, when Sallie burst in

here. It was Rosie, turning a look of pure hatred on her and saying, 'What do you think you are doing?'

It was the same face Sallie had had to endure night after night staring at her as she lay in Charles's bed; the supercilious, oh-so-high-and-mighty-look-at-me face from the silver frame. It was troubled, even a little lined, it was worried as well as angry. But it was the same face, looking down at her from a great height, as the ten-years-younger, smiling, overconfident face with its jewels. Jewels he had given her. Jewels which Sallie would like to have torn from her neck.

'Who are you?' Sallie asked.

'You know perfectly well. Get back to your room. I don't want you anywhere near my children. Do you hear that?'

That was what she said. There was no time for speech, but Sallie had said something in reply. She could no longer recollect what it was she had said, because she had gone next door to her own room. It transpired that Rosie had gone for help – was that what they were all saying? Or hidden herself? Gloria had apparently said that Rosie appeared in the kitchen in her nightdress begging them to come. Someone had said that had happened.

Sallie had gone back to her room, unravelled the rainbow jumper. Hammer. Large carving knife. Necessary tools for the finishing of a task that should have been accomplished long ago. The frenzy of it all possessed her now and she could not, when the ecstatic energy had left her, say exactly how or when or what had happened. She had the weapons, she had run back into the room, a room, found the red-haired head on the pillow, the red head lying, full of its filth and sin and lies.

As Ted's big hammer fell, she had been startled into realising her mistake. Mistake, mistake, did they not know the meaning of English?

Frances had tried to sit up. Her large blue eyes were so full of terror, and if they only knew how that had hurt Sallie, how she just wanted the terror to stop for the little girl. It was all over in a minute, she knew that. The little girl had hardly suffered at all. She did not know how so much blood could've come. It was just such a horrible accident. The red hair on the pillow. It had fallen back and the fear had stopped as down, down, down fell the hammer blows, the knife had cut the curling lips, the throat, the eyes, the hammer had finished it all in a terrible moist redness. And then the shouting, the 'Jesus!' – a man's voice, Ken's, as Sallie had felt herself being manhandled from behind and being dragged to the floor.

Now the room was so white. Sky white, tiles white. No colour, no blood, white as terror. You sat for eternity in this place.

Helstone had just gone. She thought it was only a few minutes since he'd gone. Maybe a week. It was sad that she couldn't talk any more, but now you came to think of it, that saved time. It was useful. Because, one day, she would be strong enough to stir herself and get down to writing something useful about *Turn*. There it lay, in front of her on the table, with the books Helstone had brought down from London. Not the big library copy, which would one day be hers when she went back to Bly and married Charles, but her frail little grey American paperback, the companion of her journeys. She had first read it in high school and been just so, so scared! Over the years it had been the text she had familiarised herself with the best, and it probably was true, yes, we readers change the texts we absorb. She had certainly changed *Turn*. Poor old Henry, he'd hardly recognise it, her version. Maybe that was it, maybe Hell's Bells was one of those people who thought you could get back to the *Turn* that Henry had written and maybe that could never be done. There was the old house down in the country, and the two children, and the housekeeper, and the ghosts. But they were never going to be the same again. That was certain.

The door opened. It was completely maddening, it really could in truth drive you crazy, the way they came and went in this place. Not Sallie. Oh, no, sir. There was no going anywhere for law-abiding Americans going about their business and simply trying to help people. They of course got locked up, like they had done something wrong. But these people – who was this now, in a white coat, with a kind of Chinese face, bringing a cup of something? More of those heavy drugs – they were doing their best to grind her down. It looked like some kind of meat soup, but the Chinese man said it was tea.

'You don't have to drink it if you don't want to.'

Some kind of trick, right. He appeared as if he did not care whether she drank the 'tea'. She was not going to speak. She could not speak any more. There were no more words to say, but maybe one day there would be words to write. She reached forward and opened the grubby paperback. She ignored the Chinaman who was trying to provoke her anger with his teacup.

The story had held us, round the fire, sufficiently breathless, but except the obvious remark, that it was gruesome, as, on Christmas eve in an old house, a strange tale should essentially be, I remember no comment uttered until somebody happened to say that it was the only case he had met in which such a visitation had fallen on a child.

Acknowledgements

Grateful thanks to Silas Brown, Max Egremont and
Julia Magnet who advised on terminology.

First published by Hutchinson in 2005

1 3 5 7 9 10 8 6 4 2

Hutchinson
The Random House Group Limited
20 Vauxhall Bridge Road,
London, SW1V 2SA

Random House Australia (Pty) Limited
20 Alfred Street, Milsons Point, Sydney,
New South Wales 2061, Australia

Random House New Zealand Limited
18 Poland Road, Glenfield,
Auckland 10, New Zealand

Random House (Pty) Limited
Endulini, 5a Jubilee Road,
Parktown, 2193, South Africa

The Random House Group Limited Reg. No. 954009

www.randomhouse.co.uk

A CIP catalogue record for this book is available
from the British Library

ISBN 0 09 180020 X

Papers used by Random House are natural, recyclable products
made from wood grown in sustainable forests. The manufacturing processes
conform to the environmental regulations of the country of origin

Typeset in Adobe Garamond by Palimpsest Book Production Limited,
Polmont, Stirlingshire

Printed and bound in Great Britain by
Mackays of Chatham plc, Kent

A Jealous Ghost

A. N. WILSON

HUTCHINSON
LONDON

Also by A. N. Wilson

FICTION

The Sweets of Pimlico
Unguarded Hours
Kindly Light
The Healing Art
Who Was Oswald Fish?
Wise Virgin
Scandal
Gentlemen in England
Love Unknown
Stray
The Vicar of Sorrows
Dream Children
My Name is Legion

The Lampitt Chronicles
Incline Our Hearts
A Bottle in the Smoke
Daughters of Albion
Hearing Voices
A Watch in the Night

NON-FICTION
The Laird of Abbotsford
The Life of John Milton
Hilaire Belloc
How Can We Know?
Penfriends From Porlock
Tolstoy
C. S. Lewis: A Biography
Jesus
The Rise and Fall of the House of Windsor
Paul
God's Funeral
The Victorians
Iris Murdoch As I Knew Her
London: A Short History

A Jealous Ghost

Puppet on a String. Words and music by Bill Martin and
Phil Coulter © 1967, reproduced by kind permission
of Peter Maurice Music Co Ltd, London WC2H 0EA.

547528

F

The right of Sally Spencer to be identified as the author of this work
has been asserted by her in accordance with the
Copyright, Designs and Patents Act 1988.

First published in Great Britain in 1995 by
Orion
An imprint of Orion Books Ltd
Orion House, 5 Upper St Martin's Lane, London WC2H 9EA

A CIP catalogue record for this book is available
from the British Library

ISBN 1 85797 686 X

Typeset by Deltatype Limited, Ellesmere Port, Cheshire

Printed in Great Britain by
Butler & Tanner Ltd, Frome and London

A Picnic in Eden

SALLY SPENCER

ORION